The Way to Schenectady

Maywood Public Library Rocks!!

Richard Scrimger

illustrated by

Linda Hendry

Tundra Books

Text copyright © 1998 by Richard Scrimger
Illustrations copyright © 1998 by Linda Hendry

Published in Canada by Tundra Books, *McClelland & Stewart Young Readers*,
481 University Avenue, Toronto, Ontario M5G 2E9

Published in the United States by Tundra Books of Northern New York,
P.O. Box 1030, Plattsburgh, New York 12901

First U.S. Edition 1999

Library of Congress Catalog Number: 98-60947

Canadian Cataloguing in Publication Data

Scrimger, Richard, 1957-
    The way to Schenectady

ISBN 0-88776-427-4

I. Hendry, Linda.   II. Title.

PS8587.C745W39 1998   jC813'.54   C98-931330-1
PZ7.S37Wa   1998

We acknowledge the support of the Canada Council for the Arts and the
Ontario Arts Council for our publishing program.

We acknowledge the financial support of the Government of Canada
through the Book Publishing Industry Development Program for our
publishing activities.

Design by Ingrid Paulson
Printed and bound in Canada

To Bridget

★

Thanks are cheap, so let me look like a big spender here . . .

As always, thanks to my family for support and inspiration. Thanks to my agent for resolution. More than thanks to Kathy Lowinger for direction, encouragement, and flexibility in hammering out the final draft. Thanks to Sue Tate for caring so much about clarity, and for noting – politely – the seven hundred and fifty-two glaring mistakes and oversights the manuscript still contained. Apologies (they're cheap, too) to the entire McClelland & Stewart sales force for my choice of geographical reference point. Oh, and thanks to Gracie for not biting me.

★

Some of the characters in this book may seem to bear suspicious resemblance to people in my own life, but in fact, they're all made up. The incident with the Jello-O is based on a story I heard from Tim Clarke, who ate some and lived.

1

Dinner for Breakfast

Excitement hung in the air like smoke. Smoke hung in the air, too. It was seven thirty in the morning, and Dad was at the stove frying chicken legs. Whenever we have dinner for breakfast, something exciting always happens.

"Who wants another drumstick?" He turned around, brandishing the tongs like a rapier. "Who wants another delicious drumstick? You, Captain Bill?"

Bill's my brother, sitting across from me with his mouth full.

"Wilco," he said. He can eat all day. That's why Dad asked him first. He's not a real captain, of course, but he spends a lot of time pretending to be things. Right then he was being an astronaut, and "wilco" is what astronauts say when they mean "yes."

"Good for you." Dad gave him a piece of chicken. "Now, how about some melon? Or carrots? Anyone want a carrot? You, Bernie?"

Bernie's the baby, sitting beside me with his hands full, and his diaper, too, from the smell of things. "No," he said. Bernie is almost three, and a good talker, even if he isn't toilet trained. Not really a baby, I guess, but he has been a baby for so long, it's hard not to think of him that way.

"How about you, Jane?"

That's me. "No, thank you," I said. I was too excited to eat much. What with starting our vacation, and missing Mom, and my new hair, and the beautiful summer morning outside, and Bernie's diaper, I'd barely touched my first plateful of food.

Dad frowned. "Well, drink your juice. Everyone, drink your juice. There's a lot to get rid of before we can go."

That's why we were having dinner for breakfast. Dad hates to throw out food. We always end up cleaning out the fridge before we leave on vacation. Last summer we had fried egg and spaghetti sandwiches before we left. I can still taste them sometimes.

"Drink your juice, Bernie. Come on."

Bernie obediently put his cup to his mouth. And spilled.

"That's it," said Dad, dashing over to wipe up the spill. The frying pan on the stove sputtered industriously. "You, too, Bill."

"Negative," said Bill. He's asserting himself a lot these days. It comes from being ten. I remember when I was ten, a couple of years ago. I never said "negative," but I used to say "no" a lot.

"Come on," said Dad. "We can't take half a can of juice with us in the van."

A hiss from the stove sounded like a whole herd of angry cats.

"I already have to go to the bathroom," said Bill.

"Go to the bathroom, and then come back and drink some more juice."

"Negative!" said Captain Bill.

"Just drink it," I told him. "Don't be so juvenile. It's easier to give in on the little things."

He scowled and slid down low in his chair.

"Ouch. Dad! Bill kicked me under the table!"

Bernie was pointing at the stove. "Dad! Fire!"

Dad whipped round, tried to lift the flaming pan off the element, burnt his hand, dropped the pan with a yell, and reached for the fire extinguisher.

Bill watched closely. "Remember to pull out the pin," he said, recalling last month's rocket-fuel episode. He'd found a recipe on the Internet – grass seed and oil, I think, though that doesn't sound right – and the whole mess caught fire in the basement. Captain Billy had to spend a week confined to quarters.

Only when the stove was covered in white foam did Bill leave the table to go to the bathroom.

"Isn't this exciting, Bernie?" I said.

He nodded. "I'm done my breakfast," he said.

"Good for you. Let me help you down from the chair," I said. He lifted up his arms and let me carry him away from the table. I put him down as soon as I could.

"I think I'll go upstairs and finish organizing my travel case," I said.

Dad didn't answer. He was holding a piece of chicken under running water, trying to wash off the foam. I hoped he wasn't going to make one of us eat it.

I ran to get the phone when it rang. Usually the phone is for me, and I guess you could say it was now, too, but not just for me. It was Mom.

"Hi, Mom, guess what?" I said breathlessly. "I dyed my hair." The phone is in my parents' bedroom. I checked my hair in the mirror.

4

Mom said the right thing – the thing that no one else
had said so far, not even my best friend Bridget, who
had been standing right beside me in the bathroom.
"I'm sure it looks great," said Mom. "Do you like it?"

"You bet," I said. "But no one else is very enthusiastic. Bill laughed, and Dad sighed." Mind you, he'd been
looking at the bathroom when he sighed. Dyeing hair is
a messy job. "I can hardly wait until you see it, Mom,"
I said. "I've worked out our time of arrival at Auntie
Vera's. We should be there around noon tomorrow."

"I thought you would be," said Mom. Then she
sprang a surprise on me. "You'll be in time to come to
the show with me tomorrow night," she said.

I gasped. So did the me in the mirror. "D'you mean it?"

"Just the two of us. I've got the tickets and everything. *The Music Man*, starring Ron Swoboda – whoever
he is. And the Berkshire Light Opera Tour. Their initials
are BLOT."

She laughed. I smiled into the phone at the sound of
her voice. Even though I knew she couldn't see it, I
couldn't help smiling. I felt closer to her.

"Thanks, Mom," I said. "I'll make sure Dad gets us
there on time."

"I'm sure you will, sweetie."

"How is your work going? Did you find homes for
lots of people?"

Mom's work is called social planning. This past week
she was doing it in Boston. Some kind of conference;

she goes to a lot of them. Now she was visiting Auntie Vera, who lives near Boston, in the Berkshire Hills. We were on our way to meet her there. Me and my brothers and my dad driving all the way to Massachusetts in the van. I was in charge of the maps.

"Is your dad around?" she asked.

"He's downstairs," I said. "I miss you, Mom. I'm wearing the earrings you gave me, with the little hearts on them. Do you miss me?"

"I sure do."

"No, Mom, but do you *really* miss me?" She is so busy. And the work she does is important. I sure missed her. I hoped that she missed me, too.

"Of course, I miss you. Now can I speak to Dad?"

I called him, and hung on to the phone until he picked up the kitchen extension.

"Thank heavens the fire's out," he said.

"Fire?" said Mom. "What fire?"

I hung up.

Bernie was tottering down the stairs, with a dark-colored magic marker in his hand – a dangerous weapon for a baby. I followed him quietly, so as not to surprise him.

"Give me that," I said, when he was in the front hall. He frowned. I tried to be more tactful. "I mean, isn't that a nice marker? Can I see it?"

"No."

"Please?" I said, edging closer, smiling winningly.

6

"No." He stood there, eyeing the wallpaper. Eyeing my shirt. *Oh, dear.*

"Come on, Bernie," I said. "Give me the marker."

"What?!" cried Dad from the kitchen. He was still on the phone. I could see the back of his head, where he was grabbing his hair with his free hand. "Whose idea was this?" he said.

Bill appeared at the other end of the hallway. I saw him over the top of Bernie's head.

"Bossy!" said Bernie. It's what he calls me when he's mad. "Bossy, bossy, bossy!"

I kept my distance. My shirt was new and white. "Bernie, I want you to put down the marker." I spoke distinctly, like a cop on TV. "Can you do that? Then no one will get hurt. Do you understand me, Bernie?" He glowered.

"Why do *we* have to take her?" said Dad.

Bill was sneaking down the narrow, dimly lit hall.

"Look at me, Bernie," I said. "Don't turn around. I really think you're making a mistake here. Just put the pen down. . . ."

"Two days! Easy for you, you're already there," said Dad.

"Captain Stardust, to the rescue!" Bill pounced on Bernie from behind. I took a swift step forward and grabbed him from in front. We both tried to get our hands on Bernie's wrist, but he was waving his arm wildly. In our excitement and the strength of the combined rush, we all ended up on the floor. Time passed

7

slowly, all of us struggling together. I felt something poke me in the stomach a couple of times, and heard Bill cry out once. Bernie, the baby, wriggled between us in silent, determined fury.

"Grandma's coming with us?" said Bill, his face screwed up in horror. At least I think it was. Hard to tell behind the magic-marker lines. "In the van?"

Bernie started to whimper.

Grandmothers on TV all seem to be short and fat and jolly. They make cookies and give presents and hugs. Their houses always smell like something really good is about to come out of the oven. Ours is not a TV grandma. She is long and thin and stringy. She sniffs a lot, and doesn't look at you when she's speaking. Once I heard her call Bernie a limb of Satan. I think he'd just knocked over a vase full of flowers. I asked Dad what a limb of Satan was, and if Bernie really was one. "No," he said, "it's just Grandma being mean."

"Why is she coming with *us*?" I said. "We don't like her and she doesn't like us."

"It's your Auntie Vera's idea," said Dad, with a sigh. "She thinks it'll do Grandma good."

"Why can't she take the train?" I asked. "Or walk?"

"Or stay home," said Bernie.

"You won't let me take Charles and Paul," said Bill, "because there won't be enough room." Charles and Paul are gerbils – space companions for Captain Billy Stardust. We used to call them Charles and Pauline, but after a year together it was pretty clear that we'd guessed wrong. A friend of Bill's was looking after them for us. "I miss Charles and Paul already," said Bill. "How can there be room for Grandma, and not for them?"

New England is a long way from Toronto, where we live. We couldn't drive there in a day. I had spent a lot of time with the map, and I couldn't see a way around it. We would have to stay overnight somewhere. A night with Grandma; another night without Mom.

"When are we leaving?" asked Bill.

"Right away. As soon as I clean up the kitchen. We'll pick up Grandma, and then get out on the highway. Put some real distance under our belts before lunch."

Bill and I looked at each other. "Right away" was what Dad always said. As far as he was concerned, everything was going to happen right away. In this case, right away sounded like about an hour.

Dad stared at us. Separating the three of us in the hall had been difficult – like separating eggs in an omelet – and he'd been distracted, thinking about Grandma. Now he was noticing us for the first time. "Bill, I want you to wash your face. And Jane, honey, I think you'd better change your shirt. It's covered in magic marker."

My clean white shirt. "Okay," I said, with a murderous glance at Bernie.

"Wilco," said Bill.

Bernie hung his head. He was completely free of marks. Even his hands were clean.

9

"What's for lunch?" Bill asked.

"Hard-boiled eggs and buns, and cheese sand-wiches," I said. "Two eggs each and one extra." I had helped Dad boil the eggs last night. "And apples. We'll have to remember to add one for Grandma."

Dad turned to go back to the kitchen. "And I was wondering if, maybe, someone would like to try a cold chicken drumstick," he said.

2

Blue Lady

I was mistaken. Right away was only about fifteen minutes. I had just enough time to change my shirt and comb my hair before Dad yelled that it was time to go.

"Wilco!" I heard Bill outside my bedroom door, and hurried. We ran together – neck and neck – down the stairs, out the door, and into the beautiful July sunshine. Bill beat me to the van, which meant that he got to sit in the front seat. Bernie isn't allowed to sit there – Dad and Mom are afraid he might get killed by the safety air bag. They don't seem to worry that Bill or I might get killed by the safety air bag.

"Captain Stardust in the command position of the ruby-red space capsule!" he cried. "Ready for takeoff!" Bill doesn't talk astro-gabble all the time. Sometimes he pretends to be an animal, or a tree, or a building. Sometimes he is just Bill, like in the song my Dad sings in the shower. But I think part of him really believes in Captain Billy. My brother spends a lot of time inside his head.

When he was younger, he liked to be Wild Bill, the cowboy hero. Last year he was Professor Billenstein, the nuclear scientist – until Dad made him get his hair cut.

I stood on the sidewalk, trying to catch my breath. The sliding door of the van was open. Bernie was strapped into his car seat. He was getting too big for it, and he looked like a Thanksgiving turkey in an undersized pan, spilling over the edges, waving his wings and drumsticks around. I was about to climb in beside him when I saw a brown blur out of the corner of my eye, and felt a momentary ruffling against my bare ankles.

Queenie, the little dog from across the street, had darted into the van and disappeared under the backseat. She likes our van: there's always something to eat on the floor.

No one said anything. Hadn't they seen Queenie?

"Get in, Jane, and close the door," said Dad.

"But –"

"Get in. We don't want to keep Grandma waiting."

"I really think –"

"Jane!"

I closed the door. If that's what he wanted. Dad started the car.

"Excuse me!" Mr. Timms was tapping on Dad's window. Mr. Timms looks after Queenie. As usual, he was wearing a bright golfing windbreaker and a porkpie hat, with a white feather in the brim to match his white mustache. He carried a tennis racket. Queenie loves to chase tennis balls. "Excuse me, Mr. Peeler."

Dad sighed, and rolled down the window. "Yes, Mr. Timms?"

"I think," said Mr. Timms, staring into the back, "that you might have a stowaway in your van."

"What?" Dad craned his neck around.

"A stowaway?" said Bill.

"Arf," said Queenie, from underneath the backseat.

"I tried to tell you," I said.

"I never saw her get in," said Dad. "I guess the mirrors are angled too high."

I opened the sliding door. Mr. Timms reached in and grabbed Queenie by the collar.

"Good-bye," I said to him. "Bye, Queenie."

"Good-bye," said Mr. Timms. "Have a nice trip. Don't pick up any strangers."

The van made a grinding sound when Dad wrenched it out of its parking spot. "Bye, house," said Bernie. I understood. I like to say good-bye to the house, too. It stood like an old woman, tall and thin-shouldered, with a sagging porch in the front. The flyaway shingles at the top could have been wispy gray hair. It leaned outward, as if it needed the support of the big maple tree in the front yard to stay up.

I unfolded the map and checked my watch against the van's clock.

"Are we there yet?" said Bill.

Dad glared at him.

"Just joking."

That Bill – what a kidder.

Grandma lives in a big building, with a view of another big building across the way. We don't go to her apartment very often and, when we do, we don't stay very long. That suits me fine. There are a hundred thousand little things in the apartment, and none of them is worth playing with. Some of them are pretty, I guess: painted china people – people made out of china, I mean, they don't look Chinese and they don't have MADE IN CHINA on them – and crystal animals, but if I ever pick one up, I'm told pretty quickly to put it down.

Today she was waiting for us in her living room. Her suitcase and a cooler were right by the door. She had her purse open, but she snapped it shut when we came in.

"What kept you?" she asked Dad. "I buzzed you in five minutes ago."

"Nice to see you, too, Mother-in-law." He leaned forward to kiss the air near her cheek.

Bernie pushed the button to call the elevator. He pushed it again, and again.

"The elevator isn't a dog, Bernard," said Grandma. She is absolutely the only person in the world who calls Bernie by his full name. "You don't have to keep calling it."

"What if it did come when you call?" asked Bill. His eyes lit up like the elevator call button. He loves ideas that start with "what if." "Hey, Bernie, I'll be the elevator, and you call me." He got down on all fours. "Arf," he said. His bark was deeper than Queenie's. "Arf arf!"

Bernie grinned. "Here, elevator," he called. "Here, boy."

"Arf!" said Bill, scampering over. "Arf arf!"

Grandma sighed.

She sighed again when we got inside the elevator and Bernie pressed all the buttons he could reach, which, fortunately, were only 4, 3, 2, and Ground.

"He did it on the way up, too," I said. "That's why we were late."

"Wait here, everybody," said Dad, when we got outside. "I'll bring the van around."

"Why did you park so far away?" Grandma scowled. She had two deep grooves worn into the middle of her face from all the other times she had scowled.

Dad sprinted off down the street, Grandma's suitcase banging against his leg, her cooler under his arm, his shirttail flapping behind him like a flag on a windy day.

Grandma opened her purse, put her hand in, then took it out. She frowned, closed her purse, and stared across the street.

It was hot and still. Traffic crawled up the street toward us, and down the street away from us. A regular *boom boom boom* came from inside a little car with tinted windows. The windows were rolled up, but I could still hear the bass thumping away. Bill stared at the car, mesmerized. "What if it was an animal," he breathed, "with a huge mechanical heart?"

Four more years, I thought. In four more years, I'll be old enough to drive. The car rolled down the street toward the intersection, and the sound of the radio faded into the day. We waited on the sidewalk. Not much to say. Bernie was bent over, looking at bugs. Bill had his head turned, to watch the car as it turned the corner.

"Do you like my hair, Grandma?" I said, just to make conversation.

She looked startled. I couldn't tell what she was thinking. "That's right. It *is* different, isn't it?"

"I think it's ugly," said Bill.

I stuck out my tongue at him. Childish, I know, but I couldn't help it.

"Look," said Bernie. He held up his hand. On it was a beetle.

"Oh, dear," said Grandma. She took a step back from us. Now I could read her thoughts as easily as the headlines of the newspaper: *Two days in a van with them? I must be crazy.* She opened her purse again. This time she found what she was looking for. She took out a cigarette and lit it with a plastic lighter.

Bernie smiled at the bug on his hand, and then bent down to place it carefully on the grass at the edge of the sidewalk.

"What are you staring at, Bill?" Grandma sucked greedily on the little white stick. Smoke drifted out of her nose in a lazy gray stream. Bill blushed and looked away. We'd both spent hours in school watching videos about what happens to your lungs when you smoke. I didn't want to think about Grandma's lungs.

"I see a blue lady," said Bernie. He's not really sure about his colors yet.

A bus passed by. People walked by. Everyone going someplace. Some of them had briefcases; others had knapsacks. One old man, with a beard like Santa Claus, pushed a baby carriage filled with junk. He smiled at us as he passed. Bernie smiled back. Grandma didn't.

"So that's what's keeping your father," she said, peering down the street. She started to laugh. With the cigarette in her mouth, she looked like a fire-breathing dragon.

I followed her gaze and saw Dad talking – Bernie had got it right – to a blue lady. A policewoman. Dad's hands were in the air, pleading. She had a notebook in her hand, and an expression of complete and utter disbelief on her face.

It was a time for action. "Come on," I said. "We have to help."

"Why?" said Grandma.

I stared up at her. *Didn't she care?* "Because he's getting a ticket. He's in trouble." I turned to my brothers. "Come on! Let's help Dad."

"Your father told you to stay here," said Grandma.

"This is an emergency. Come on, guys!"

"Wilco!" said Bill.

"Dad said . . ." Bernie began, but Bill and I each grabbed one of his arms, and ran with him bumping between us.

"Hey!" That was Grandma behind us. "Bernard, William, Jane, come back!"

We kept running. Grandma's shrill voice followed us, like a lost soul searching for a home. Looking back, I saw her – not running, exactly, old people don't run – but moving as fast as she could. "Wait for me," she called. "I'm coming, you little baskets!"

I think that's what she called us.

3

Point for Me

We clattered up to the van in a fury of footsteps and loud breathing.

"Oh, hi," Dad said to us. He looked embarrassed.

"Are we in time?" asked Bill. "We came as fast as we could."

Bernie wiggled his arms. We must have pulled them almost out of their sockets. "I came even faster," he said.

The policewoman smiled and kept writing.

"Better get in the van, children," said Dad, in a resigned way. "This won't take very long."

Bill slid in to the very back of the van. I helped Bernie into his car seat, and sat beside him.

Grandma came hurrying up, her eyes burning more fiercely than her cigarette. "Well, this is a great start to the vacation."

"Oh, hello, Mother-in-law."

"Nice parking job. A long way from the front door, and illegal, too."

Dad sighed.

"Don't mind me," said Grandma to the police-woman. "No one does. I haven't mattered to anyone since my husband died. Just another lonely old lady. Keep writing the ticket, officer."

"But don't take away his license," I said. "We're driving to Massachusetts to see Mom."

Grandma was in the front seat, with the window unrolled. "His name is Alexander Peeler. He lives on Garden Avenue with my younger daughter and these three urchins. Big old house, plenty of room. Needs a coat of paint, though, and a new roof, but he's too cheap to fix it up." She spoke with grim enjoyment.

The policewoman's expression had changed since we showed up. From being kind of bored and uncaring, she began to look almost, well, compassionate. She stuck her finger in her notebook, marking her place. She spoke to Dad, "This old lady with a mouth full of lemons – you're driving her to the States?"

"Yes, ma'am," said Dad.

"Long trip," said the policewoman. "I'm sorry for you." That shut Grandma up.

"Sorry enough to tear up the ticket?" Dad asked.

"No."

But she stood out in the middle of the road and stopped traffic so we could pull out of our illegal parking spot. Dad called "Thanks" over his shoulder, but the policewoman was already writing another ticket.

We edged forward in silence for a moment. I think we were all surprised at what Grandma had said. Even she was surprised.

"Dad," (predictably, Bernie was the first of us to react) "what's an urchin?"

"A mop-top, gap-toothed, knee-high rebel," said Dad promptly. "A ragged, freethinking, contemptuous answer to the sour complacency of an older generation." He turned his head. He wasn't smiling. "Isn't that right, Mother-in-law?"

She didn't say anything.

"Wow," said Bernie.

The highway would be coming up soon. I opened my travel case.

"About what I said back there," began Grandma in an undertone.

"We've got a big house, do we?" said Dad, speeding up to get onto the highway. "Big enough for what, you lonely old lady?"

"Forget I said anything. Please. I'm in a lousy mood today. I don't know what I was thinking."

I couldn't remember hearing Grandma say "please" before – not even "please pass the potatoes." She'd say, "If you're quite finished with the potatoes, Jane, maybe someone else would like to have some." That's not please.

Bill's voice was a plaintive whine, the sound of a cheap remote-control car trying to climb a ramp. "Are we there yet?" he said. I guess he couldn't stop himself from asking.

My brother is good at parsecs and microns. These are not the measures on our road map. I folded the map and held it out to him. "See, Bill," I said, "we're here, in Toronto. See, I've circled it. And we're going to Auntie Vera's, which is just outside of Pittsfield, all the way over here," I unfolded the map, "in Massachusetts. Do you see? I've circled that, too. There's the scale of the map down at the bottom. On average, we travel the length of my thumb every hour. We have to travel eighteen thumb lengths before we're finished." I folded up the map. "Now do you see, Bill?"

"Negative," he said grumpily.

"Shall I explain it again?"

"You know, if this really was a spaceship, we'd be there in eighteen seconds. Whizz!" he said suddenly, in a loud voice, startling Grandma. "Whizz! Bang! Boom! And we'd be there!"

Beside me, Bernie squirmed in his car seat. "Maybe we'll be there *soon*," he said. "Soon" is what Dad usually says when we ask "Are we there yet?" Bill and I are old enough to understand that he doesn't mean it, but Bernie is just a baby, and he still feels better when he hears it. "Will we be there soon?" he asked.

"Yes, Bernie," I told him. "We'll be there soon."

He smiled. He's got all his teeth now. Cute little baby teeth like a row of milk-white corn niblets. "Don't worry, Bill," he said, throwing the words like salt over his shoulder to avoid the bad luck. "Jane says we'll be there soon."

"Not soon enough," said Grandma.

As we turned onto the highway that would take us out of the city, Bill lurched sideways and hit his elbow. He started to whimper, very dramatically, and I told him to, well, I told him to shut up. He got angry and leaned forward to *boomp* me on the head with his fist; I may have accidentally undone my seat belt, turned around, and knelt on my seat in order to *boomp* him back. Accidentally. And he screamed and started to complain, and I called him a name, and he called me a name, and, before we knew it, Dad had pulled out a bag and started throwing candies around the car. "And do up your seat belt," he told me sternly, with his mouth full of toffee.

"Ouch," said Bill, when the toffee hit him in the nose. I giggled. He bounced out of the seat and bonked me on the back of the head. I screamed. He giggled.

Overhead, the sun was beating down. In the van, Bernie was beating on the front of his car seat. "Go faster," he said. I knew how he felt. The faster we went, the sooner we'd get there. I thought about Mom, checking her watch at Auntie Vera's. I started to hum "Seventy-six Trombones."

Lots of cars all around us. The highway had about fifteen lanes, and they were all full. Where do the people go? It was ten o'clock on a midsummer Monday, and people were sure anxious to get somewhere. The same cars seemed to appear and disappear, no matter how fast we went. The same faces behind the steering wheels: grim faces, work faces, busy faces.

"Let's play a game," I said. I love to get people organized so they can have fun. If the game lasted for an hour, it would be time to think about lunch. "How about the game where we get points for the things we see? Do you know that one, Grandma?"

She didn't answer.

"Do you remember that game, Bill?"

He didn't answer.

"Remember, Bernie?" I asked, poking him. "Remember we'd get points for seeing cows or horses? Or barns? Remember, Bernie? Cows, point for me?" Usually, he likes my suggestions. But he didn't answer either. He had that faraway look, deep and mysterious. Either he was about to have a nap, or . . . "Dad," I whispered, "I think Bernie's making a diaper."

Dad was offering Grandma some coffee from the cup that sits on top of the thermos. She was shaking her head.

"What?" he said. "A diaper? Bernie, don't you remember what we talked about after breakfast? And yesterday? Don't you want to be a big boy? You said you'd try to remember to tell me before you had to go."

Bernie looked guilty. "I'm fine," he said. "Now."

I moved away from him on the seat. I knew what that meant.

Dad made a gesture of impatience. "I can't understand you, Bernie. I can't understand why a boy, who speaks in sentences, who can remember things from last year – a boy who can practically tell time, for crying out loud – why that same boy cannot tell when he has to go to the bathroom."

Bernie shook his head. He couldn't understand either.

We were slowing down. Hot air shimmered over our hood. All around us were cars steaming gently in the morning sun. The highway was like a giant pot, filled with boiling eggs. Would one of them pop?

"I should have had the van serviced," said Dad. "The temperature gauge doesn't seem to be working. Either that, or we're running a little hot."

"Cows," said Bernie.

"That's it. Point for you! Good!" I said. He remembered from last year, on our way up to the cottage. In fact, there were no cows now; we were in the middle of the suburbs. Off the highway were places that sold tires, and places that sold rooms for the night, and places that didn't sell anything, just sat there in rows like empty boxes. You couldn't get to them from the highway even if you wanted to, and I couldn't see why you'd want to.

"My turn," I said, peering through the windows one at a time. "I see a big apartment building, but I don't think that's worth a point. I see a church in the distance. And – oh, look!" I said, staring through the windshield. Up ahead was a truck turned sideways, blocking one lane of traffic. One of its doors had popped open, and I could see a cow's head sticking out.

"You were right, Bernie," I said. "Cows."

"They say 'moo,'" he confided behind his hand.

"Do they?" I said.

"Moo," he said.

"Moo," I said, as deeply as I could. It sounded just like a cow to me.

"Moo," said Bill, from the backseat.

"Have a candy," Dad said to Grandma.

"I do not want a . . . candy," said Grandma. I must say, by the way, that Grandma has another nasty habit besides smoking. She swears. I'm not allowed to say those words, so I won't repeat them, but Grandma uses words that rhyme with "shell" and "ham" a lot. "I don't want a ham candy," said Grandma.

We were passing the truck now. Very slowly, one car at a time. The cows stared out at us as we passed by. They were almost close enough to touch.

"Mooooo," we all said together. Bernie was laughing so hard, it didn't come out right.

"Stick of gum?" Dad offered to Grandma.

She shut her eyes. Her hands were trembling. "Take it away," she said, in a low voice. "Take it away, I tell you, and leave me the shell alone!"

"Elephant," said Bernie. "Point for me."

"Where?" I asked, peering around.

He opened his blue blue eyes really wide. "In the zoo," he said.

4

A Huddle of Old Clothes

We took the next exit off the highway, and drove down a road with hardly anything on it except signs showing how to get to other roads. Asphalt ramps snaked all around us. In the distance, huge power pylons marched across the landscape like giants. "Are we there yet?" asked Bill, not very hopefully.

"We're outside Oshawa," I told him. "There, see." I held out the map, but he wouldn't look. We stopped at a gas station. Dad told us we could get out and stretch our legs, then grabbed Bernie and the diaper bag. Grandma already had her door open, and was reaching into her purse. Bill and I climbed out more slowly.

"There's a vending machine," I said.

Dad and Bernie disappeared toward the washrooms – Bernie under Dad's arm, wriggling. Grandma stood beside the van.

"You can't smoke here, ma'am," said the gas station attendant.

Her face fell.

"Not near the pumps, ma'am. It's a regulation."

She moved away from the van and lit her cigarette in the shade of a stack of old tires.

Bill and I bought ourselves cans of pop from the vending machine, and wandered around behind the gas station. We could hear the sound of the highway – a constant whine.

"Do you have to go to the bathroom, Bill?" I said. "It'll be another hour and a half until we stop for lunch."

He stuck out his tongue. I sipped my pop. Root beer.

And then a pile of clothes spoke to us. At least that's what I thought at the time. A huddle of old clothes heaped against the back wall of the gas station.

"Oh, no," it said. Or possibly, "Oh, woe." I wasn't paying close attention to the choice of words. The idea of an animated pile of rags was more interesting than what it was saying. The voice went on, "So thirsty. So far to go. How am I going to get there?"

I shrank back against Bill. I'd heard of people who could make it sound like something across the room was talking. Throwing their voice, they call it. I wondered if someone was throwing his voice into a pile of dirty clothes.

And then the pile sat up. And it wasn't laundry anymore. It was a man.

A small, bumpy-faced man, with white hair and white eyebrows that went up in little points, like paper hats, or that French accent I can never remember the name of.

28

A small, skin-and-bones man, with a hole in one of his running shoes. A crinkly-eyed man, who climbed to his feet with effort, as if it were a long way up – which it wasn't – and stared at us.

A stranger. They keep telling us about strangers in school, and it would be hard to imagine a stranger stranger than this one. I was surprised to see him appear from nothing, but I was more surprised than scared. Maybe because he was smaller than I was. Maybe because he'd been crying.

"Hello," I said.

Bill's mouth was open. No sound came out of it.

"Do you . . . want some root beer?" I asked the stranger.

His chin moved sideways when he ducked his head. A tiny man, with nervous, jerky motions, like a bird's.

"You said you were thirsty." I put the can in his hand and watched him drink. His fingernails were long and dirty. He finished my root beer and licked his lips.

"Thank you," he said. "Thank you very much. When one person shares, two are enriched." A smile flickered across his face like summer lightning. A good smile. I felt better, seeing the smile, knowing it was for me. I felt I had done something worthwhile.

"I'm Jane Peeler," I said.

"Thank you, Jane Peeler. I'm Marty Oberdorf." He had an old man's voice, high-pitched and thin.

"Pleased to meet you." I shook hands. His was dry and firm.

"And this is my little brother Bill."

Bill shook hands, too. "Nice day," he said.

Marty started to cry again.

Usually I hate it when grown-ups cry. So embarrassing. Bridget's mom cried during the movie *Titanic*. Like it was a surprise the boat sank. I was sitting with Bridget, and we both pretended we didn't know her. But, somehow, Marty crying wasn't so bad. He wasn't much of a grown-up – however old he was, he wasn't any bigger than we were. And besides, I'd already helped him.

"What is it?" I asked. I was going to put my arm around him, but then I thought I wouldn't.

"My little brother is dead," he said.

30

I didn't know what to say. "I'm sorry," I said finally.

"We weren't friends," he said. "Not since we were kids. He got married, and started a business. I went traveling. I've been all over the world. And I was in Toronto yesterday . . ."

"We're from Toronto," said Bill.

"And I saw a newspaper from home. From New York. And it had my brother's picture in it. I hadn't seen him in years. He looked good in the picture: handsome, respectable. An important man. It was like I was seeing him, really seeing him, for the first time. And, do you know, I was proud of my brother."

Well, of course, I knew what was coming.

"And he's dead," said Marty, his eyes filming over. "That's why his picture was in the paper. He's dead, and the family is having a memorial service for him."

Bill offered Marty the rest of his pop. An unusual gesture for Bill. Usually when he offers you something, it's because he doesn't want it, or because there's a worm in it.

There was a big trash container nearby. Marty tossed my can into it, and took Bill's. "I haven't been home in years," he said. "I want to go to the service, but I don't know how I can get to Schenectady. I have no money. I tried to hitchhike, but no one would give me a ride. So I walked. I walked all day. I got here last night, and I fell asleep. And now I will never get home in time." He swallowed, which was funny because he hadn't taken a sip of Bill's drink yet. "It's just as well," he said. "I am different. I'm not like them. I'm a failure. They wouldn't want to see me. How could I face my brother's wife? My nephews? Big strong men, my nephews. My brother was big, too. I was always the runt."

An idea was coming. That's how it works for me. Some people go out looking, as if ideas were gold, or the Northwest Passage. Not me. I get bitten by an idea, as if it were a bug. The idea finds me. This one flitted over the surface of my mind, a mosquito that wouldn't land. Here was somebody who needed to get home. Could I . . . could we . . . I wondered if . . .

Marty reached into a pocket and pulled out a crumpled sheet of newsprint. "I tore out the article," he said.

I didn't look at it. There wasn't time. "Schenectady," I said. "I know that city from the map. It's in New York State. Isn't it?"

Marty nodded.

"Near the Massachusetts border?"

He nodded again.

"We are driving to Massachusetts," I said.

Bill's eyes widened. He knew what I was thinking. "Dad wouldn't even let me bring the gerbils along," he said in a whisper. "Marty is a lot bigger than a gerbil."

"We won't tell Dad," I said.

If Bill's eyes widened any more, they would roll right out of his head and go *splat* on the pavement. "How are you going to get away with it?" he asked.

Marty was following our conversation anxiously, his

32

head snapping back and forth as if Bill and I were playing tennis. "What is going to happen?" Marty asked.

"Do you want to go to your brother's memorial service?" I said. "Do you want to go home?"

"Yes," said Marty. He swallowed again.

"Good," I said.

We didn't have much time. Dad would be finished with Bernie's diaper by now, and Grandma with her cigarette. We had to move right away.

"I mean, no," said Marty. He turned away, and slumped against the wall.

A thought struck me. Getting Marty home would take time. Not too much time, because Schenectady was practically on the way to Auntie Vera's. But my plan was adding hours to our trip. How many hours? I'd told Mom we wouldn't be late.

Now, suddenly, I didn't want to take Marty with us.

"You know what he is?" said Bill in a whisper. "You know what Marty is, really?"

"No," I said. I was ready to go back to the van without him.

"He's an alien," said Bill.

"Yes," Marty agreed. "I am an alien. That's exactly what I am."

"An alien from . . . Schenectady," Bill said, savoring the last word. "What a great sounding place. Anything could come from Schenectady."

33

I took the newspaper clipping from Marty's out-stretched hand, and read it quickly. Tobias Oberdorf had died at the age of sixty-eight, which struck me as awfully old to be someone's little brother. I wondered if Marty had ever thought, when he was my age, that his little brother would someday be old enough to leave a grieving widow, Marie; a son, who was an ex-Mr. Olympia New York State; and a whole bunch of cousins, who were prominent in the church community. And that was not all.

"Listen to this," I said to Bill. "'An elder brother, Martin Oberdorf, passed long ago from the family circle, but not from our hearts,'" I read. "'Old wounds can still be healed.'"

Marty groaned.

"We've got to get him home," I said to Bill, putting the clipping in my pocket.

It was the right thing to do. When you know something is right, you have to act on the knowledge, or else you're not doing the right thing. Mom said that. Come to think of it, Mom's job was all about getting people homes.

I so want to be like her. That was why I'd dyed my hair last week. My own hair is dark, like chocolate, and Mom's is almost red: chestnut, she calls it. And the label on the hair dye in the drugstore read CHESTNUT RED TINT. "I have to try it," I told Bridget, who frowned at the other dye we were considering – purple – and said, "I thought chestnuts were brown."

If Marty slowed us down, well, Mom would have to wait. I was pretty sure we'd still be in time for the show.

"Get up, Marty," I said. "You walked all the way here. Of course you want to go home."

"But I'm no good. They don't want to see me."

"We're going to get you home," I said. "We're going to get you to –"

"Schenectady," said Bill. He loved the word. His eyes lit up. "His native planet! Schenectady, the world of Oberdorfs."

I was glad that Bill was enthusiastic. My plan couldn't work without him.

Marty sniffed.

"Listen, both of you," I said. "Here's what I want you to do."

I was relieved to see Grandma stubbing out her cigarette when I got round to the front of the gas station. A lot of time seemed to have passed since we'd stopped. Dad and Bernie were struggling in the middle seat of the van, trying to get the seat belt over Bernie's shoulders. I sauntered over casually. I wanted to look behind me to check that Marty and Bill were in position, but there was no point in making a plan and then not following it. I kept walking.

"Help!" A bit faint, but it came from the right spot. "Help!" Louder now, with more feeling in it. "Help, Dad! Help, Grandma!"

Now I risked a look – not at Bill, who was stuck to the barbed-wire fence on the far side of the gas station – but behind me. Marty peered around the corner, by the washroom door. So far, so good.

"What the . . ." said Dad, somewhere between alarmed and angry.

"Help!" Bill sounded like he was in trouble. And, of course, he was in trouble because he's not supposed to climb on other people's property. He hadn't wanted to do it, but I needed a diversion, so he agreed. He knows that there are times when he has to do what I say. After all, he's my little brother. I suppose it'll be the same when I'm seventy and he's sixty-eight. Right then he sounded as if he was about to fall off the fence.

"Hang on, Bill!" shouted Dad. He abandoned Bernie and hurried toward the fence. Grandma was moving, too. All according to plan. The sliding door of the van was open. I climbed in and stood over Bernie.

"Let me strap you in," I said. "Then we'll play hide-and-seek." My plan was to give Marty the signal when Bernie covered his eyes.

"Okay." Bernie liked hide-and-seek. "You hide your eyes first," he said.

That wasn't part of the plan. "No, Bernie. You hide yours first."

"You."

"YOU."

"YOU!"

"Bernie," I said. I could see Marty edging out from the cover of the gas station. A small man moving carefully. "Bernie," I said, "let's do it my way. There isn't much time."

"NO."

My plan was starting to unravel. Bernie wouldn't shut his eyes. I looked around and saw, to my horror, that two strangers had got out of their jeep and were hurrying over to help Bill. An elderly couple. White hair, white shoes. Shirts with flowers on them. The woman was clutching a half-eaten donut. The man reached up and grabbed Bill's ankle.

"Careful, Henry," called the woman.

My plan unraveled further. Dad stopped running. Bill was putting up a fight, but the man was stronger. He had Bill by the legs now.

"Come on down, son," he said.

"Thanks!" Dad called out, checking over his shoulder to see what Bernie was up to. "Thank you so much!"

"Isn't it providential that we decided to stop here for gas?" said the woman.

I clenched my teeth. It *wasn't* providential at all. Grandma was heading back to the van. My plan wasn't going to work. All I'd done was waste time and get Bill in trouble. Through the window of the van I saw Marty stop. His shoulders slumped.

Grandma had her hand on the front door. Dad

marched to the van, looking relieved and angry. Bill shuffled slowly after him, looking apprehensive.

Another idea bit me – just a little bite, a fleabite of an idea. I moved fast.

"What was that click noise?" Bernie asked me.

"I don't know," I lied. *Don't run away, Marty*, I thought. *Stick around for another minute. Just one more minute. We'll drive right past you. Just wait.*

Grandma got in. Dad got in. Bill got in. Dad started the engine, and drove away from the gas pumps.

The light in the roof of the van stayed on. The warning bell rang. The robot voice that comes from the car company told us that a door was ajar.

Dad stopped the van.

5

Something Stinks

"Check your doors, please," said Dad. He tried his. Grandma tried hers. The light stayed on. The alarm kept ringing *ding ding ding*. A helpful diagram of our van was lit up on the dashboard.

"It's the back," I said, pointing behind me. "It's open."

"How on earth did that happen?" asked Dad.

Because I pushed the release button myself. But I didn't say that out loud.

"I'll close it," I said, opening the side door and climbing out.

Bill stared at me.

We were stopped right beside the gas station. I swung the big trunk door open wide. Suitcases, bags full of laundry, and beach toys reached almost to the roof. I stood on tiptoe, but couldn't see over them.

"Jane!" called Dad. "Can you close the door?"

"Sure," I said. "I'm just arranging our stuff back here."

Marty was at my elbow. I shoved a bag out of the way, making a space in our trunk area. Good thing he was so small.

"Do you want help?" Dad said.

"No," I said.

"Can I have something to eat?" asked Bill.

"No," said Dad. "I'm upset with you."

Bill sighed.

"Can I?" said Bernie.

"Me, too," I said. Bill turned around to glare at me from the middle seat. Dad tossed a package over his shoulder. It flew all the way to the backseat, landing in my lap. Mints. I tore open the package and leaned forward to give one to Bernie, dropping one by accident in Bill's lap.

"Thanks," said Bernie.

Bill thanked me with his eyes.

"Feeling better, Mother-in-law?" Dad asked, maybe because she was leaning more comfortably against the back of the seat.

"Better than what?" She frowned at Dad.

We drove on in minty silence.

"Horsies," said Bernie, pointing. I turned. Horses, all right. We had left the suburbs behind, and were out in farm country. The horses stood in the middle of a field, with their heads down, eating grass so green it looked plastic. The red barn in the background looked plastic, too.

"Good, Bernie," I said. "And what do horsies say?"
"I want another mint."

In the car, nothing happens sooner than you think it's
going to. You imagine everything long before you see
it; you anticipate it, think about it, consider it from all
sides, and then – only then – does it loom on the horizon:
a cloud no bigger than your hand, but the rain's still a
long way off. I'm talking about lunch. We'd been driving
for what seemed like hours and hours and hours. I was
hungry. Worrying about Marty, thinking about all the
things I wanted to tell Mom, organizing games – these
things tired me out. But when I checked my watch, it
was only eleven thirty. No way were we going to stop for
at least another half hour. I went over the lunch routine
one more time. I knew where the picnic hamper was,
and what was in it. I knew where the bag with the sunscreen and bandaids was. I knew where all the hats
were. What else would we need for lunch? Drinking
boxes? In the hamper. Handiwipes? In the diaper bag
and the sunscreen bag.

And on the subject of diapers . . . no, it wasn't quite
like a diaper. But there was something. I wondered what
it could be. Familiar and strange at the same time. Not
pleasant. Not pleasant at all. I was in the very back seat.
It was coming from behind me. A very peculiar . . . a
very pungent . . . I guess you'd have to call it a kind
of . . . well, a kind of . . .

"Something stinks," said Grandma.

Marty. I guess if you hadn't had a bath in a while, and you were wearing clothes you'd slept in for a few nights, you'd start to smell a bit. It wasn't so bad in the open air behind the gas station, but in the van, with the windows closed, Marty was free to tell his own story.

Bill was sitting in the middle seat beside Bernie. Bernie was walking his stuffed monkey back and forth along the arm of his car seat. Bill turned around and looked at me anxiously. He recognized the smell all right.

I craned my neck so I could see over the back of the seat, but there was no sign of Marty. He was buried beneath our pile of gear.

"I don't smell anything," I said.

"I do," said Bernie. "But I don't know what it is."

"I . . . don't smell anything either," said Bill. "Mind you, I have a stuffy nose."

What a coward. I glared at him.

"Let's open a window," I said. "That should freshen things up."

Bill opened his window. I opened mine. Unfortunately, van windows open only about an inch. I guess the designers don't want kids falling out.

After a minute Grandma said, "It still stinks back there."

"You're right. Yuck. It's almost like something died," said Dad.

Bill and I looked at each other. "What if there is . . . a body in the car?" Bill asked. I gasped, but he went on

42

quickly, "An alien body from the planet Schenectady – I mean, from another planet?"

Dad smiled. I breathed a sigh of relief.

"Look!" I pointed to a road sign. "Odessa is coming up." I reached into my travel case to find my map, and pulled out a square package. Not my Walkman, which I usually keep there, but the bottle of cologne that Bridget had given me for my last birthday. I kept it on my dresser. I couldn't remember packing it. I must have put it in the case instead of the Walkman.

A lucky mistake. The bottle came with a sprayer. I pointed it at the ceiling of the van, and pressed down. And again.

A minute later Bill turned around with an expression of disgust on his face.

"What?" I whispered. "What?"

"Perfume?" He wrinkled up his nose. "What do you call that stuff?"

"Summer Nights," I said. Actually, it smells kind of nice.

"Yuck," he said.

"Better than Eau de Marty," I whispered.

It took a little while for the perfume smell to spread through the van. We passed Odessa. Bernie fell asleep.

"Smells different in here now," Dad commented. "Less like a morgue, more like perfume." He tapped one of the gauges on the dashboard. "Hmm," he said.

Grandma sniffed critically. "Charnel Number 5," she muttered.

43

Dad laughed. Bill and I exchanged a relieved glance. The pavement changed. The wheels had been saying *origami, origami, origami.* Now they started saying *Tweedledee, Tweedledee, Tweedledee.*

"Almost time for lunch," I said.

"Yes, when's lunch?" Bill asked.

Dad sighed. "Next picnic area we pass, we'll stop."

"I can hardly wait," I said.

The wheels went back to saying *origami, origami, origami.*

Bill turned around in his seat belt. "What if Marty gets thirsty? Or has to go to the bathroom?" he whispered.

I shrugged.

"What if he suffocates? Goes into a coma? What if he dies?"

Bill has such a morbid imagination.

"What if no one finds out he's there," I whispered, "and, thanks to us, he arrives in Schenectady and gets reunited with his family?"

"Someone will notice," said Bill, turning away and closing his eyes.

"You know there's a spider over your head," I said. Bill didn't open his eyes, but he was paying attention. I could tell. "It's on a little thread of spiderweb attached to the seat-belt hook. Now it's letting itself down on a thread," I said softly. "Getting closer to your face."

Bill won't admit it, but he's really scared of spiders. Me, I like them – even the big, hairy kind. It helps that they're girls. I know we've got something in common. My friend Bridget and I formed the Spider Club in school last year. Bridget believes in reincarnation, and she's convinced that she was a spider in a past life.

"The spider is right over your face now," I said to Bill. "Can't you feel the little legs brushing your cheek?" He couldn't help himself. He squirmed out of the way, shuddering all over. Of course, there was no spider on the ceiling.

"Just kidding," I said, with a light laugh.

He leaned back and punched me.

"Ouch!" I said.

"Just kidding," he said, with a nasty chuckle.

The next sign at the side of the highway was a picture of picnic tables. LAKE VIEW it said underneath. "Dad, Dad, Dad!" we cried together. Bernie woke up. "Dad!" he said, even before his eyes were open.

"I see it," Dad said.

"I'm hungry," I said.

"Me, too," said Bill and Bernie.

The noise of air rushing past our inch-open windows dropped dramatically. The car was suddenly quiet, poised, expectant. I don't know about the boys, but I was thinking about hard-boiled eggs.

"Hungry," said Marty, into the hush of awakened appetite.

Bill almost twisted his neck off, turning around so fast. I stared at him helplessly. The only thing I could think to do was cough.

"Something caught in my throat," I said. I tried to make my voice sound like Marty's – high and thin, and a bit raspy. "Sure am hungry," I said again.

"Me, too," Bill said. "I'm hungry, too."

"I'm going to start with a hard-boiled egg," I said, "and then go on to a cheese sandwich. And an apple. For dessert –"

"I brought the dessert," Grandma said. "Made it myself this morning."

"Great!" said Dad heartily, turning onto a gravel road lined with painted wooden fence posts. In a moment I saw the lake, like the sign told me I would.

"Great," Bill and I echoed, very faintly.

I leaned back casually, and dropped the rest of the package of mints over the back of the seat behind me. They would help Marty stave off hunger until we could figure out a way to feed him.

6

"You Shouldn't Have!"

I must say, reincarnation sounds like a great idea. I wonder if I could come back as an owl because they get to stay up late, and they never have to do any science homework. Maybe Grandma could come back as a cook. No way she's ever been a cook in any long-ago past life. Make that any of her lives at all, including this one.

Fortunately, I have not had to eat many meals at her apartment. She's not very – is "hospitable" the word I want? Sounds like it might mean something else, something about being sick, but whatever the word is that means being a good hostess and making sure everyone is having the time of their lives at your place, Grandma isn't that.

Last time we were there for dinner was ages ago, and dessert was a pale gray confection, like a shovelful of cement poured into a loaf pan and left to harden. *Charlotte russe* she called it, speaking with some kind of accent. Mom and Dad smiled grimly, and Bill and I dug in because it, well, it smelled like it might be sweet anyway. I don't know what nationality Charlotte was, but she couldn't make dessert. The stuff stuck to my fork, then my hands, then my mouth. Days later I was still digging pieces of it out with my toothbrush. Bill started quickly, but even he didn't finish his plateful. Lucky Bernie, he got to eat vegetables out of a jar.

I had to figure out a way to get food to Marty. We parked in a shady spot. The picnic hamper was under the backseat. While the others were getting out of the car and finding a picnic table with the best view, I slid out the hamper and opened it. I hunted around inside for something to give Marty. The sandwiches were wrapped up together. I found an egg and took it out.

"Psst, Marty," I whispered. "Do you like eggs?" And, of course, that's when Dad appeared at the door.

"What are you doing, Jane?" he asked.

"Getting lunch ready," I said.

"And why are you holding that egg?"

I held it up. "This egg . . . um . . . made a noise. Like the chick inside was pecking its way out. I was wondering if it was alive. I was worried about it."

"Jane, that's a hard-boiled egg," he said.

"Oh, yes," I said.

Dad was staring down at me. I was on my knees on the floor of the van, wrestling with the picnic hamper. "Are you feeling okay?" he said.

"Fine," I said. "Just fine."

I pulled the hamper toward me and, at that moment, I heard Marty again.

"Egg," he said loudly.

"– scuse me," I said, quick as a flash. An inspiration. "Egg-scuse me, Dad," I said. Loudly. "I burped."

"I didn't hear you," said Dad.

"It was only a little burp," I said.

"Let me carry the picnic hamper," said Dad.

"Egg!" said Marty again.

"– cellent idea," I said quickly. "An excellent idea, Dad. Here, let me slide it over to you." I was thinking hard, racking my brain for useful words.

"Are you . . . well, Jane?" Dad asked. "It's pretty hot."

"Egg!"

"– stremely hot," I finished for Marty. I was ready for that one. "But I think I'm okay. Let's get out of here, Dad. Before I start –"

"Bacon!" said Marty. Surprisingly.

I wiped my brow. "I mean, before I start baking to death! Whew!" I said.

Dad tucked the picnic hamper under one arm and put the other one around my shoulders. "You sure you're feeling okay?" he said.

"You bet."

So we all sat down around the table with the best view, and got out hard-boiled eggs and cheese sand- wiches and buns and juice boxes. There wasn't any

49

chicken; I looked. Later I asked Dad what had happened to it, and he said he'd tried it and it tasted awful, even with the fire extinguisher foam washed off.

It was a busy meal for me. I had to invent reasons for going back to the van. Sunscreen, lip protector, map – and once, I said, because I wanted to check myself in the mirror. Dad stared and shook his head. I don't usually forget things. I don't usually have four eggs and two buns and two cheese sandwiches for lunch either. And three juice boxes.

"Pig," said Bernie, as I reached into the hamper again.

"Could you put your plate in the garbage bin?" I asked him.

"Bossy pig!"

It was worth it to know that Marty was going to be okay for the next little while. "Thank you, Jane," he told me when I brought the cheese sandwich. "Food in a hungry belly takes away fear."

Bill was acting normal – for him, that is. The ground was quicksand, he claimed, and with every step he sank deeper and deeper. He bent over, walked on his knees, crawled.

I finally got him alone. "Crawl up to the van," I whispered, "and give this bun to Marty."

He was kneeling in a soft bowl of pine needles, near a rocky promontory. The sun was bright, but it was cool by the lake. He shook his head. "Negative, sir. I'll sink over my head by the time I get there. It's just suicide." He sounded serious. Did he believe himself? Had he forgotten about Marty? Hard to say with Bill.

Grandma turned away to light a cigarette and lost the last half of her sandwich to an aggressive seagull.

"Ham those birds," she said, but without any real bad feeling.

"Have another sandwich," Dad offered.

"There's no more," said Bernie. "Jane ate them all."

"Have some more grape juice."

"I don't want any grape juice."

"Have some cheese," I said.

"She doesn't want any ham cheese," Bill told me, in a gravelly Grandma voice.

We laughed. Dad told us to behave ourselves, but I could see there was a smile behind his stern expression, the way the sun is there behind the clouds even if you can't see it directly.

"Very funny," said Grandma. I couldn't tell if the sun was there or not. Some clouds are darker than others.

"What's for dessert?" asked Bill.

Grandma smiled grimly and opened her cooler. Took out the single dish. Laid it on the picnic table. And we all stared.

It lay on the middle of the picnic table, wobbling back and forth.

"I made it myself," she said.

Bill took a step backward and sank to his knees. I didn't know if he was praying, or if he'd just landed in the quicksand.

Dad said, "Mother-in-law, you shouldn't have."

She didn't answer. She was looking better than she had in the car. More relaxed. The cigarette in her mouth probably helped.

Grandma had a big spoon in her hand. "Who wants the first serving?" she asked.

Silence.

Well, would you speak up if what you'd be getting was the first serving from a Jell-O mold in the shape of a fish? Stop, let me get this right. It was a fish – a wiggling, wobbling sea creature made out of lime-green Jell-O, with a poached egg in the middle where its heart would be.

"It's alive!" said Bill. "Hey, it really *is* alive." He prodded it with his finger.

"William!" said Grandma. "Hands off!"

A shiny black jeep pulled in to the picnic area. In it was an elderly couple. By the time the old lady emerged from behind the wheel, the old man had already unloaded deck chairs, checkered tablecloth, and barbecue grill.

Bernie climbed to his feet and pointed. "Flower lady," he said.

Nobody paid attention. We were mesmerized by the dessert. I could hardly take my eyes off it. Glints of sunlight flashed on the edges of the mold. The fins moved back and forth, as if the fish were swimming in an unfamiliar element. A dessert to remember for the rest of our lives.

Dad's smile was wide. If I didn't know him so well, I'd swear he was actually enjoying the moment. How can grown-ups lie so convincingly? Practice, I guess. "What an astounding creation," said Dad.

Well, that wasn't quite a lie.

"It looks 'ucky," said Bernie.

That wasn't a lie either. He put his hands behind his back as if he were afraid the fish would snap at him.

"Mind your manners," said Dad. "Grandma worked hard to make you this . . . incredible dessert. You must be polite."

She swung the serving spoon like an executioner's ax. All our heads were on the block.

Help, I thought. I wanted something to happen. I didn't want to eat the dessert, and I didn't want to hurt Grandma's feelings. I didn't want to lie either. Mostly I didn't want to eat the dessert.

Birds wheeled overhead, graceful and raucous. There was a large cloud coming up fast from across the lake, but it looked too puffy and white to be a rain cloud.

Grandma raised her hand. Dad's smile wavered. Bill swallowed nervously. I hid my eyes. I do it when I watch TV as the heroine's friend is about to go into the room where the "Thing" is waiting for her. There was a sudden screeching, closer and louder than usual, and a flurry of activity. I peeked through my fingers and saw, to my surprise, a huge white bird on the center of the table. I couldn't understand it. Then I realized that the lifelike dessert had been mistaken for a real fish, and been pounced on by a roving seagull, who was, naturally enough, confused. Hard to pick up a Jell-O mold in your beak.

The bird was noisy, angry, and soon gone. In its wake lay the mangled remains of what had been a fish, bleeding bright yellow blood from its heart.

"Did you see Grandma hit the bird?" whispered Bill. "With her hand?"

"No, with her spoon. *Whack!* Right across its head."

The old couple from the jeep came over, with sympathetic smiles. "Hello, again! You folks all right?" the woman asked. Flowers on her shirt, like Bernie had said. It took me a moment to recognize them as the people who'd helped Bill down from the gas station fence.

"Fine, thank you." Dad turned with a smile. "A seagull took exception to my Mother-in-law's dessert."

"Pretty darn bold," said the man.

"I thought it was an angel from heaven!" said the woman. "Swooping down in white like that! I said to Henry – this is Henry, by the way, and I'm Myrna. We're

from upstate New York, on vacation until we saw yesterday's newspaper – I said to Henry, 'That looks like
an angel of God!' Only he said, 'It's a bird, Myrna.' He's
the practical type. I'm always more spiritual. I do parish
work back home, St. George's Episcopalian, and I often
see the Hand of God in earthly events. When my
lumbago started acting up last fall, I had to stay in bed,
and a tree branch fell right across our front walk; might
have killed me if I'd been outside, which I wasn't. Do
you see the Hand of God in earthly events, ma'am?" she
said to Grandma.

"No," said Grandma.

"You folks want some donuts?" said Henry. "We
bought some on the highway. More than we can eat. Be
happy to share."

"Henry, what a marvelous idea! It's so like you to be
generous to people like these. People in distress. People
in need."

"Donuts." Bernie and I looked at each other.

"Alien cuisine," said Captain Billy.

"Too bad they're across the quicksand," I said.

"It's my duty to try them," said Bill. "On my knees,
if I have to."

"A kind offer," said Dad. "But we couldn't take
advantage –"

"Nonsense," said the lady. "I was saying to Henry as
we bought them, 'Are these donuts really necessary?' We
don't need them. So it's almost as if they were meant for
you folks. The Hand of God again."

As if to underline her words, the puffy cloud rolled in front of the sun, and the sky darkened momentarily. We made our way toward the other picnic table. The wind was picking up, ruffling the edges of the checkered tablecloth.

"Thank you," I said to the man. Henry.

"You're welcome, my dear. Say, did your brother hurt his foot climbing that fence?"

I turned. Captain Bill was on his knees, struggling through the quicksand.

7

A Jet Plane Taking Off

I grabbed a couple of donuts – carefully choosing the ones without icing sugar – and waited for an opportunity to get back to the van.

The kind old lady, Myrna, wouldn't let me go for the longest time. She babbled on about how much I reminded her of one of her grandchildren; we had the same perky smile and good manners, the same – ugh – sparkling wit. What do you say to something like that? "Thanks," I mumbled, my mouth full of donut.

"Of course," said Myrna, "Emma's hair is dark, like my daughter's, and yours is . . ."

"Chestnut," I helped her.

"Is it really?"

"Like my mom's."

"You and Emma have so much in common. I really think the two of you would get along like a house on fire."

Finally she left me alone. I saw an opportunity and snuck back to the van, getting the surprise of my life when I saw Marty sitting up in the seat.

"What are you doing?" I whispered. "Get your head down. We'll be leaving soon."

"Oh." He frowned. "Right."

I gave him a donut.

"I know that man and woman," he said. "Where do I know them from?"

"The gas station," I said. "They were at the gas station."

"Were they?" He crawled back into his hiding place.

I put a bag of clothes on top of him. "Sorry," I said. "Now, remember, when we get going, don't make a sound. Not a sound. Do you understand?"

"Actually, I am kind of tired. I'll probably go to sleep," he said.

He wasn't the only tired one. As we pulled out of our picnic spot, Bill yawned and Bernie wore that folded-in look. He was in that place where babies go before they fall asleep.

"How many donuts did you have?" Bernie asked me.

"I don't know – one or two," I said.

Grandma turned around in the front seat to look at me.

"Or three or four," I said quickly. I'd forgotten the ones I put in my pocket for Marty.

"Hog," said Bill from the backseat. This was for Dad's sake. He knew I had taken them for Marty.

"Am not," I said. "And anyway, how many donuts did you have?"

"Only two."

"I had five," said Bernie sleepily.

"Hog," Bill and I said together. Bernie smiled smugly and settled back in his car seat. A happy hog.

Dad put one of his tapes in the deck. *Oklahoma!* Bernie fell asleep. The car filled with music. The highway and the afternoon stretched out ahead. My eyelids started to droop. I heard Dad and Grandma talking in the front.

"Go on," he said. "I don't mind, and they're all asleep."

"No," said Grandma. Her voice sounded a little tight.

"I'm not asleep," I tried to say, but the words fell together like a stack of cards toppling to the floor. My head rested against the window.

When I woke up, yawning, the car smelled of smoke.

"Is there a fire?" I asked.

Grandma looked out the window.

"There was," Dad explained over his shoulder, "but it's out now."

The man at the border crossing leaned out of his booth and asked us where we were going and why, and for how long. Then he asked our names and how old we were. He wanted to know if I liked ice hockey, which I sort of do, and if Bill spoke French, which he sort of doesn't. I expected a snort of impatience from Grandma, but she kept her temper very well.

"That's all then; enjoy your holiday," said the man,

waving and returning to his booth. There was no one behind us.

"He suspected us," I said, "didn't he? He asked a lot of questions."

"He was just lonely," Grandma said.

How she could be so sure? I thought back to her apartment. It is pretty small, too, like the man's booth, and there isn't a lot of traffic going by. She must feel like that man a lot of the time.

Grandma hadn't always been lonely, of course. She and Grandpa used to live in a house with a hill in the backyard, and roses under glass jars in the garden. I was little, barely older than Bernie is now, and Bill was just a baby, and Grandma would say things like, "Have you finished with that section of the newspaper yet?" And Grandpa would say, "No." He was very old, and spent most of his day on the couch.

Before that Grandma had Mom living with her. She wouldn't have been lonely then. I'm never lonely with Mom. It's nice when it's just the two of us, which it isn't very often. We go out to lunch and put on lipstick and talk about the things we would do if we had a million dollars. On the way back home from lunch, we stop for a swing in the park. And then we go home and have a cup of tea. It's not as exciting as when I'm with Dad. Nothing burns down. Nothing breaks. I never have to run, or shout, or save anyone from drowning. But it's really, really nice. We're the only two girls in the house, after all.

60

I wish Mom was around more. I read once – it was in the doctor's office – about a man with a hole in his heart. Actually, I think the article was "Man with Hole in Heart Rescues Baby from Inferno." The man looked normal, but he had this teeny pin-sized hole in his heart, which, he said, made him feel empty – not all the time, just sometimes. I really identified with that man because I feel empty, too, sometimes, as if my heart has a hole in it where Mom should be. Sounds stupid, I know, and selfish because I have a Mom, and she does important things. I get to see her. Just not as much as I want.

Odd to think about Grandma feeling lonely. I'd always figured that she enjoyed leading an ornery cornery life all by herself. But I guess being mean and grumpy is just a habit. A bad habit, like smoking.

Grandma isn't going to quit smoking.

We drove in silence through the pretty countryside. Soon we were in hills, up and down, with the sun sinking behind the ones on our right. "How's our schedule, Jane?" Dad asked me. "Should we look for a place to stop soon?"

"Not yet," I said. "It's only four o'clock." The farther we went today, the earlier we'd get to Auntie Vera's tomorrow.

"Did you reserve a place to stay?" Grandma demanded.

"No," said Dad.

"Why not?"

"This is Watertown," I said. "We could get to Sackets, or even Pulaski."

"Relax, Mother-in-law. Be flexible. Be open to new experiences."

Grandma didn't say anything. I was working out how long it would take us to go from Pulaski to Schenectady, and then how long from Schenectady to Pittsfield, when Marty started to snore. Or maybe he didn't start; maybe he'd been snoring all along. But he started snoring *loud*. I knew what it was as soon as I heard it: a piercing, high-pitched rush of air.

For a second no one said anything. "Bill?" Dad darted a look over his shoulder. The van swooped like a swallow. "Bill? Is that you?"

I turned around. Bill was doing his best to help. He lay still in the very back seat, with his eyes closed and his mouth open, pretending to snore. I thought hard.

"Maybe . . . maybe we shouldn't wake him," I whispered.

Another snore. Another swoop. "He sounds horrible," said Dad. "Like a jet engine taking off. It can't be healthy. Bill! Hey, Bill!"

Darn. I thought again. "I don't feel well," I said.

It hurt to say it. If we stopped now, even for a few minutes, we'd stay the night. We wouldn't keep going to Pulaski. We'd be that much further behind schedule. I gritted my teeth. "I have to go to the bathroom," I said.

Marty taxied down the runway again.

"Oh, Oh, Oh. I really have to go," I said.

"That rhymes," said Bernie. "Doesn't it?"

"There's a hotel!" I shrieked. "I see it."

"You know, I think I would like to use a bathroom, too," said Grandma.

"Not me," said Bernie. "I don't need one."

"All right." Dad slowed down and changed lanes. "I guess we can stay here," he said.

I relaxed – slightly. All I had to worry about now was getting Marty out of the van without anyone seeing him.

8

Dead Body

Grandma was helpful when we were getting ready to unpack the van. Dad wanted to carry our bags up to the housekeeping suite we had rented for the night, but she insisted on seeing it first.

"I think Grandma's right," I said. "Check out the rooms. You, too, Bill and Bernie. I'll be along in a minute."

"I thought you had to go the bathroom," said Dad.

"The feeling passed," I explained. "You know how it does sometimes."

Dad frowned at me, but he led Grandma upstairs. Bill and Bernie followed, and I followed them – just as soon as I'd popped the trunk and released Marty. He woke up slowly and groggily.

"Where are we?" he asked.

"Watertown, not too far from Schenectady. You have to go now," I said. "But I want you to meet me back here tomorrow morning at seven o'clock. The parking lot. Seven o'clock. Okay?"

He nodded.

"You'll have to find your own place to sleep," I said. "I have an American five-dollar bill in my wallet. Do you want it?"

He nodded.

"Will you recognize the van?" I said.

He nodded. "I've been under plenty of them," he said.

"Sleeping?"

"No – repairs. I worked in a garage. Mind you, I've slept under them, too."

"Oh."

He yawned. He didn't look much worse than he had this morning, but he'd looked pretty bad this morning. Before closing the trunk, I had to ask one thing. "Uh, Marty, you didn't . . . while you were in the back there, you didn't . . . you didn't have to . . . go to the bathroom, or anything," I said. "Did you?"

He didn't say anything.

I closed the trunk and ran upstairs.

It was like an apartment. There was a tiny kitchen, a living room with a prickly fold-out couch and a balcony, and two bedrooms – one for us kids, and one for Grandma. Dad eyed the prickly couch unhappily. Both bedrooms had locks. Dad put towels over the tops of the doors so that no one could close them by accident and lock themselves in a room without a key or a grown-up. Once in Orlando Bill and I had closed the adjoining door on Bernie, who was by himself in Mom and Dad's room along with the wallets and keys. Dad had not forgotten.

I didn't unpack except for my toothbrush and pajamas. I zipped up my suitcase again, and put my travel case on top of it.

Bill already had his bathing suit on. And his mask and snorkel. And fins. Diver Bill, ready to explore another alien environment.

"There's no pool here," I said.

"Sure there is, Miss Smarty-pants. This is Watertown, right?"

"So?"

"So hotels come with pools. Pools of water."

"Gee, what do hotels come with in Washington? Washing machines?"

He frowned behind his mask.

"In Denver, do the hotels have dens?" I asked. "In Helsinki, do they all have sinks?"

He was trying to frown, but he couldn't keep it up. "Maybe. And guess what they have in Hamburg?"

"Or Bombay?" I said. "Or Flushing Meadows?"

"Cows," said Bernie, bouncing up and down on the bed. "Point for me." There was a picture on the wall, with cows in it.

"We're not playing that game anymore," I said.

"Dad," Bill called to my father in the other room, "is there a pool in this hotel?"

"Sorry, son."

"Told you," I said.

"Oh, dear," said Grandma. She was outside on the little balcony. "There's a dead body."

"Point for Grandma," said Bernie.

I went outside on the balcony. It smelt like rain was coming. From up here on the second floor, I could see a bunch of cars rusting quietly in a gravel lot. None of them had any tires. On the other side was a billboard advertising a career in the army, BE ALL THAT YOU CAN BE.

Not an attractive view, and the body didn't help. It really looked dead. I've seen enough of them on TV to know what they look like. Shapeless and small, a pile of old clothes lying on the ground. There was a newspaper covering its head. When it blew away, I thought I'd faint.

Oh, no. Oh, no. It was Marty – lying there and not moving. He'd collapsed. Was he . . . I felt ill. I felt like I was about to cry.

Grandma stood beside me. I could smell the powder she puts on. Old lady smell.

"There, there," she said.

Her words didn't register. The first kind ones I could remember my grandmother saying to me, and I was too preoccupied to notice. "Is he really dead?" I said. "Maybe we should check."

I watched closely. A breeze came up to ruffle Marty's clothes and the newspapers beside his head. It began to rain. I felt it. So did Marty. He moved. He struggled up into a sitting position, then used a rusted car to lean on while he pulled himself to his feet. I sighed with relief. He reached into his pocket and took out the donut I'd given him.

"Jane, are you all right?" The rain beaded like diamonds in Grandma's fine silver hair.

"Yes, I'm okay," I said. "I'm great."

Bill came outside to check. "Is it really a – hey, wait a minute." He'd recognized Marty. "Isn't that . . ." His voice trailed away.

"What?" asked Grandma.

"Nothing," said Bill.

Marty wandered away. From up here he looked even smaller than usual.

"Come on," I said, dragging Bill inside.

I don't understand Mom when she says how sick she is of hotels. I couldn't get sick of hotels if I lived in them forever. Imagine an eternity of room service, of wrapping all the big towels around you, of bouncing on all the beds, and never having to tidy up. Imagine an eternity of roast chicken dinners in a fancy dining room, with cream gravy and mashed potatoes, and ice cream sundaes for dessert. I can hardly bear to think about it – it's too beautiful.

Ah, well, I determined to make the most of my own heavenly moment in the Watertown Inn. "Butterscotch sundae," I said to the waitress, who gave me a smile and said she understood, dearie, and would make it herself, extra specially, with all the hot butterscotch sauce she could find.

"Chocolate sundae," said Bill, avidly. He licked his lips in anticipation.

"I feel sick," said Bernie.

"Too sick for ice cream?" I asked incredulously. He nodded.

Dad reached across the table and put his hand on Bernie's forehead. "Hot," he said.

I felt my own forehead. Some of my hair had come out of the barrettes I use to keep it in place. I repinned it.

"Is Bernard going to be sick?" asked Grandma.

Dad ignored her. "Jane, Bill, I'm going to take Bernie up to the room. Okay? You stay here and eat your ice cream. Come on, Bernie. Come with Daddy." He gathered him up in his arms. The way Bernie's head flopped against Dad's chest and the way his little arms went instinctively around Dad's neck told me, more clearly than any thermometer, that he was a sick little guy. "Night night," he said to everyone. His cheeks were red. His eyes were closed.

Then the waitress came with the ice cream, and I forgot about Bernie. The whole world came down to a white china bowl, a teaspoon, and a mouthful of delight. Paradise passed in a waking dream of sweet fulfillment.

"My goodness, William, anyone would think you were in a race," said Grandma.

I looked up absently. Bill, of course, was finished his dessert. Grandma frowned at him over an almost full cup of coffee.

"Can I go?" he asked.

My bowl was barely touched. No point in hurrying through paradise. I always eat slowly. Why wait all afternoon for dinner, and then toss it down like a couple of aspirin?

"Can I go back to base now, Grandma? I mean, to the room?"

"By yourself?"

"Affirmative," he said. "There are clear markers. I'll be fine. I know where it is. I'm ten years old, for heaven's sake."

She waved her hand. "Make sure you go straight up to the room." He saluted and disappeared – another dangerous mission for Captain Billy. I went back to my dessert. More time passed.

The restaurant was in the downstairs part of the inn, a big room with plants on the ceiling and a row of windows. From our table you could see the street. Imagine my surprise when, as the last melted drips of ice cream and butterscotch were gliding slowly down my throat, I glanced up at the windows and saw a familiar face.

Grandma was on her feet. "Jane, that's it. You're finished. I don't think they'll have to wash that bowl now. Or the spoon. They can just put them back in the rack and use them again on another ice cream lover."

"What's Bill doing out there?" I said.

"Where?"

"Out there. He was at the window beside that empty booth . . . just a second ago. Then he walked away down the street."

Grandma frowned, piling a whole rack of V-shaped wrinkles between her eyes.

"Should we go and get him?" I said. "He's probably lost." For an interplanetary explorer, Bill gets lost very easily.

The waitress came up. "Is something wrong?" she asked Grandma.

"It's Bill," I answered for her. "He's outside and he may be lost."

"Your brother? The chocolate sundae?"

"Yes."

"Door's over there," she said. "I'll take care of your check. What room are you in?"

Grandma blinked. "I don't remember," she said.

"Neither did Bill," I said.

9

Not Quite Romeo and Juliet

When we got outside, there was no sign of him. "Come on," I told Grandma, and pulled her down the street.

"Where are we going?" asked Grandma.

"We're following Bill," I answered. "I think he got lost on his way to the room. So he left the hotel and is now walking around it, trying to find the room from the outside."

"Why would he do that?"

"Because he's Bill. Why would he eat a chocolate sundae in two bites?"

Grandma couldn't answer that one.

"I don't think Bill could be here," she said. We were around the back of the hotel, in a fenced-off area with parked vans and garbage cans and a smell I recognized as lobster bisque. I'd had it as an appetizer less than an hour before.

"You're probably right," I said. Then, over top of the wooden fence, I saw the same billboard I had seen earlier that afternoon. BE ALL THAT YOU CAN BE. Pictures of people in jeeps, in tanks, in parachutes. In control. The girl driving the jeep had no hair.

The window of our room was nearby, but where? I was pulling Grandma toward the end of the fence when I heard Bill's voice. I froze. So did Grandma.

"Help!" Bill shouted. "Help me, Dad!" It came from up ahead of us. We hurried toward the sound.

Dad's voice was fainter than Bill's, but audible. "Bill!" he shouted. "Where are Grandma and Jane?"

"I'm lost!" shouted Bill.

"What?" shouted Dad.

"I'm lost!" shouted Bill. "Lost. I can't find the room."

"Where are Grandma and Jane?"

"I don't know. Can you come down and get me now?"

"I'm locked out!" said Dad. "The balcony door slammed shut on me when I came out, and now I can't get back in to the room. Come up here and get me out!"

"I can't" shouted Bill.

"Why not?"

"Because I'm lost!"

Grandma snorted. I looked up and saw a ghost of a smile on her face.

"Men," I said, under my breath.

"You said it, missy."

We came to the end of the fence, and found ourselves in the gravel lot full of rusting cars. Sunlight had faded at the end of the long summer day. No automobile traffic. No pedestrians. The streetscape behind the hotel was deserted, except for Dad and Bill shouting at each other. Dad was bending over the rail of the balcony, and gesturing extravagantly. Bill was looking up, with hope beginning to give way to doubt. Not quite Romeo and Juliet. Neither of them noticed us right away. Grandma stopped to look at one of the rusted cars.

"Okay. Go around to the front door," Dad was shouting at Bill. "And tell the woman at the desk to come up here right away with the key."

"Come up where?" said Bill. "What's the room number?"

Dad's mouth opened wide. I could see his pink tongue gleaming from two floors down. "Don't *you* know either?"

"Bill!" I called. "Dad! We're here!"

"Jane!" Bill whirled around. Tears mingled with the chocolate syrup on his face. No longer the intrepid Captain Billy. Just a little lost boy in a strange town. "And Grandma. Am I ever glad to see you!" He ran toward us, gave me a hug, then threw his arms around Grandma. She looked startled. Tentatively she put her arms around his shoulders.

"Jane!" Dad was waving at us. "Helen!"

A first. I can't remember the last time Dad called her Helen. She didn't blink.

"Where's Bernie?" I called.

"He's sleeping. I can see him through the window. But I'm locked out. Can you come and get me please?"

"I don't have the room key," called Grandma. "You took it, remember?"

"Get another one from the desk."

"Yes, but what room number are we?"

75

Dad stopped and stood still for a second. "You don't know either?" he said.

"Of course not."

"Doesn't *anyone* know what room number we are?" he shouted at the heavens.

I couldn't keep it in any longer. "211," I said.

Bill sighed.

"Thank you, Jane," said Dad. "You are the girl with brain. Now get another key from the front desk and let me back in to the room."

"Okay."

"People actually live in these abandoned cars," Grandma commented as we passed. "There are blankets and sleeping bags and tins of food."

"That's too bad," I said seriously. I thought about having a rusty old car for a home. Not what they dreamed about in social planning. At least Marty had a real home to go to.

"Yes," said Grandma. "It *is* too bad."

"You know," said Bill, as we made our way down the gray carpeted corridor past room numbers 208 and 209 and 210, "these doors all look the same."

I didn't say, *Well, duh*. Restraint. Instead I nodded sympathetically. "Sure do," I said. Bill frowned and punched my arm, which is usually what he does when I say, *Well, duh*. Seems as if I can upset him just by being polite. Of course, I was in an incredibly superior position.

The desk clerk, a perfumy lady who nodded while she talked, opened 211 for us, and nodded us all inside. Bernie was asleep in the middle of the big double bed.

Dad was staring in at us, his face pressed to the glass of the balcony window. He looked funny. Bill and I burst out laughing when we saw him. The desk clerk looked startled, like she wasn't used to kids laughing at their father. Bill ran over to let him in.

"Thank you," said Dad. "It's a nice view, but you can get tired of it after a while."

"On behalf of the Watertown Inn, I'd like to apologize for your inconvenience," said the desk clerk, nodding earnestly. Dad smiled and said the shoe was on the other foot. "On behalf of the Peeler family, I would like to apologize for the inconvenience to the management."

Grandma sniffed. "I'm a Collins," she said.

The desk clerk smiled nervously. "Well, if everything's okay now," she said.

"Everything's just fine."

"And if you decide to go out again later this evening, I'd suggest taking two keys," said the desk clerk.

Dad looked like he wanted to say, *Well, duh*. He didn't. "Good idea," said Dad.

It started to rain again. Bill found a science show on TV. Grandma muttered something about going downstairs for a breath of air. Dad said, "Why not have your breath of air here?" but Grandma shook her head and headed out the door. I assumed she was going to get some tar and nicotine with her oxygen and nitrogen and whatever else there is in our air. Bernie woke up feeling much better. He and Dad played a gentle bouncing game until Bernie hurt his elbow. Dad gave him a cold cloth, and picked up the phone.

On the TV a man in a white coat and thick glasses was giving us some unlikely sounding facts about crystals. Bill was ecstatic. It's not all make-believe for him; he loves science, too. One of those boys with chemistry sets and singed eyebrows. He's never happier than when he's waiting for something to go off.

"Yes, you could say we've had an eventful day," said Dad into the phone.

"Who is it?" I whispered to him.

He was smiling. He moved his lips to make the word "Mom." He listened to what she said, still smiling.

"Let me talk to Mom," I said.

"Mom?" Bernie was bouncing on the bed again. He held the cold cloth to his elbow. The ends of the cloth dripped water as he bounced up and down. "Let me talk to her. Let me!"

Smallest first is the rule in our house. I sighed and went back to the TV. Very suspicious, these science shows. I understand what they are saying, but I don't believe a word of it. Bill was rapt. I wished I had a peanut, to see if I could throw it into his open mouth.

"I'm better now," said Bernie into the phone very fast. "Daddy got a ticket. I fell asleep. A bird ate Grandma's dessert!"

It's exciting, and a bit sad, to hear your mother's voice on the phone. She's Mom, and she's far away. "Hi," I said.

Mom called me honey and said I was the heroine of the hour for remembering the room number. I could feel her warmth through all the length of phone cord.

"I miss you," I said.

She said she missed me, too.

"I'm looking forward to *The Music Man*," I said.

She said she was, too.

There was a question I wanted to ask her. "Mom, do you think it's sad if someone gets separated from his family?"

She didn't reply right away.

I went on. "If someone is separated from his brother, then he should try to get back and see him, shouldn't he?"

"Brother? Are you and Bill having a fight?"

"Oh, no," I said. "I'm talking about someone else. And if the brother is dead," I went on, "the other brother should try to get to the funeral. Or the memorial service. Shouldn't he?"

"Jane, honey, what's going on?"

"I just wondered what you thought, Mom. It's all about doing the right thing. I'm glad you agree with me. I think he should go, too. Even if it's in Schenectady."

Mom asked if she could speak to Dad.

"Hang on," I said. "Bill wants to talk to you first." He was standing at my elbow. "Bye, Mom," I said. "I love you."

"I love you, too," she said.

I woke up in the middle of the night because I heard a noise. "Who's there?" I whispered. The curtains were drawn and it was as dark as the inside of your pocket. "What's going on?"

"It's Grandma snoring." Dad's voice came from the living room. "Go back to sleep."

I listened. Sure enough, I could hear a faint sound like a distant waterfall. Not unpleasant. "Sounds kind of soothing," I said. I lay back and pulled up the covers. Then the sound stopped. I waited and waited. My lungs hurt, and I found that I'd stopped breathing. After an eternity the waterfall started again.

"Wow!" I said.

"It's the waiting that gets to you," Dad said. "I'm having trouble sleeping, too. Mind you, this couch isn't helping."

"Can't you close the door to her room?"

"It *is* closed. If she just snored regularly, like your mother, that would be fine. But the sound stops and I lie here waiting."

"I didn't know Mom snored," I said.

"You used to crawl into bed with us when you were

little. Don't you remember? You'd hit your mom to make her stop."

I had a sudden memory of my parents' bed. Not a picture, a sort of sense memory. I couldn't see the scene, but I could remember the warmth of their bodies after the cold hallway, and the smell of the pajamas and sheets. I closed my eyes and smiled into the past. And then, I couldn't help it, I felt a prickle at the corner of my eye. I closed my eyes, and let the tears slide down.

10

And I Was Happy to Have Her

I've read more than one book where the heroine has a
foolproof method for getting up on time. If she wants to
get up at seven, she turns round seven times before
getting into bed, or says a special prayer to her guardian
angel or the saint of the morning, whoever that is – not
St. Kellogg of Battle Creek – or sleeps so that her body
is in the seven o'clock position of the bed. Or something. My infallible method is an alarm clock. I've had
the same one for years: a digital display in a bright red
case, with seventeen jewels inside. It says so on the dial.
Only my alarm clock wasn't foolproof this morning
because when I got up, it said 7:45. I must have forgotten to set it when I went to bed.

Everyone else was already up. How could I have slept
in? I bounced out of bed and went over to the mirror.
Dad was drinking coffee. He brought his shirtsleeve up
to his face. The shirt was wrinkled, and so was his nose.

My hair looked okay – a little flat, but okay. Splashing
came from our bathroom. "Who's in there?" I asked.

"Bill wanted an early-morning swim. He's taking a bath in his bathing suit and snorkel."

Marty, I thought. *Got to find Marty.* I was already late for our meeting.

"When are we leaving?" I said, brushing my hair.

"Right away," said Dad, the way he usually does. "After you have breakfast. Bernie's eating and watching cartoons in Grandma's room. She's out having a smoke."

"Is something wrong, Dad? You look upset."

"This shirt smells awful. I'm sure it was clean when I packed it."

I decided to wear yesterday's clothes.

Bernie was in his pajamas eating a cheese Danish. I estimated that "right away" was going to be about fifteen minutes. I dressed in Grandma's bathroom, took one Danish from the plate, and wrapped another one in a napkin.

"I have to go down to the van," I called to Dad.

"Wait!" He came into the room. "What are you doing?"

"I have to get something," I explained. I made it deliberately vague, and looked down at the floor.

"Oh." I'm almost thirteen and Dad thought he understood. "Oh, okay," he said, handing me the car keys.

"Thanks, Dad." I ran. *Be there, Marty*, I thought. *Be there, be where I can find you.* It was a fine, fresh, summer morning, with a little bit of a breeze to rustle the flags at the used-car lot across from the hotel, and shake last night's rain from the trees. I checked the van – he wasn't there. I even checked inside the van, thinking he may have found a way past the door locks, but he hadn't. I ran around the hotel parking lot, breathing hard, cursing myself for oversleeping and Marty for not waiting, checking underneath all the cars and trucks. Nothing.

I stood in front of our van and called his name loudly: "Marty!"

Echoes rang. Birds flapped. Nothing else. I tried again, even louder: "MARTY!"

Got a strange look from a passerby. I gave it one more try, filling my lungs, stretching my vocal chords, not caring who I disturbed, as long as I disturbed: "MARTY!!!!!"

"Jane, there you are!"

I jumped. "Bill, you startled me."

My little brother, frowning, wet-haired. "What's going on? Dad and Grandma are wondering where you are. We're getting ready to go."

"Bill, something terrible has happened. Marty has disappeared. I arranged to meet him here at seven o'clock, and . . . he's gone. I've looked all over the parking lot."

"That's too bad. Mind you, Marty did smell, didn't he? Now, come on upstairs."

I stared. Was Bill just going to give up? "We have to find him," I said. "There isn't a lot of time. He could be anywhere."

Now it was his turn to stare at me. "Did you say *we*? And *have to*? And *find him*?"

"Don't you care about him at all? You cared yesterday. Planet Schenectady, remember? You helped me get him into the van. You pretended to snore so he wouldn't be discovered."

"That was different. He was right there, and, well, he looked sad. Now he's gone."

"Bill, help me. I helped you find Charles and Paul when they escaped from their cage."

"I keep telling you, Marty is not a gerbil."

"I helped you move your whole room around so the bed would be on top of the grape juice stain you made on the carpet."

"And I gave you my dessert for a week."

I'd forgotten that part. "Well . . . I didn't tell your friends when you started getting phone calls from Irene," I said. "I didn't even tell Bridget, and she would have told everyone in the school."

He blushed. Got him. "Okay. Okay. I'll help."

"Great. Thanks, Bill. It'll be an adventure."

He smiled, finally, and saluted. "Tell me what to do. Captain Billy Stardust is at your service. Or, even better, I could be a tracking dog. A bloodhound. That's what you want, isn't it?" He made his mouth droop like a hound's, and dropped to all fours. "Awooo!" he bayed.

"Bill!"

"Awooo! Good thing Marty's so easy to sniff out." That Bill. I had to laugh.

"Go up and tell Dad I feel lousy. Say that the two of us are going to take a walk around the block together, to clear my head. Then come back down." I knew we'd have to go together because Bill would be sure to get lost on his own. "I'll wait for you."

"Awoo," said Bill, and disappeared.

I was staring up and down the street, wondering where in the wilderness of a strange town to start my search, when an idea bit me. Marty knew about cars. He might remember what our van looked like, even if he forgot where it was. Across the street from the hotel, under flapping plastic flags, was a used-car lot. To Marty it might look like a hotel parking lot, especially if there was a bright red van, a few years old, parked a few rows in from the road. Was there?

It would take only a minute to find out. I ran across the street and found not one, but three, vans the same color and style as ours. And under the third of these, sound asleep, was Marty. He squawked like a startled pigeon when I pounded on the red fender.

"Get up," I said. I grabbed hold of his dirty shirt. "Get up!"

"I know you," he said, "you're the egg girl." He tried to roll over.

I pulled him out from under the van. "Quick!" I said. "Follow me."

"Wha-at?" Marty's pointed eyebrows climbed slowly up his forehead. He seemed dazed. He smelled different than yesterday. Not better, just different. I hauled him upright – he weighed more than Bill, but not much more, and I could still carry Bill around – and dragged him across the street. When we got to the van, I was sweating. He was gasping.

"This is a V-6, isn't it," he said.

"Here." I thrust the cheese Danish at him.

"I recognize the vehicle. Seen a few better years, it has." He nodded. "You know, this parking lot looks different, somehow, in daylight. Where are the flags?"

"Across the street," I said. "Last night you slept across the street."

"No," he said. "I was right here. Under this van." He yawned.

"Eat your breakfast," I said.

"Thank you. When you feed the body, you feed the soul."

Footsteps pounded on the concrete. Coming closer. I tensed. "Awoo! Awoo!" I relaxed. It was only Bill, the hound of the Peelers. "Awoo! Aw –" He stopped when he saw us. "You found Marty," he said. He didn't sound very enthusiastic, I noticed. "I brought Dad's suitcase," he said, "and ours, and the diaper bag."

"Thanks, Bill. Put them in the trunk now." I unlocked it from the outside. "What about Grandma's case?" I said. "Could you get it, too?"

He frowned at me. "What am I? A slave, and you boss me around?"

"Please, Bill."

"Yes, boss lady, I will go and try to find the other

case." He shuffled off, taking little steps, as if his legs were chained together.

"Better get in," I said to Marty.

He finished off the Danish and wiped his hands on his pants. "Why?" he said.

"So you can go to Schenectady." Now that I'd found him I wanted to get moving. The memorial service started at two o'clock. Should be plenty of time, but you never know. And the sooner we dropped off Marty, the sooner we would get to Auntie Vera's. "Schenectady. Where your brother is. Remember?"

He swayed a bit. He must have been so tired. "Poor Tobias," he said. "My poor brother." He started to cry.

"There, there," I said. "But, really, Marty, you have to hurry."

"I can't go back. They don't want me."

"They do so," I said.

"Tobias and I had a big fight years ago. I left home and never came back. Tobias made millions selling real estate. I had trouble finding work as a musician so I started to drink too much. I drove cabs, and worked in garages. I drifted around. Since last year I've been living on the street. I thought about calling my brother, about going home, but somehow I never found the way to Schenectady."

I couldn't think of anything to say.

"I'm scared, Jane. They're rich and important and I'm just a freak. An old broken-down singer, who can't hold a job."

"I didn't know you were a singer," I said.

He sniffed back his tears. "Bars, nightclubs. Nowhere special."

"Hey! What are you doing?" a voice rang out.

I turned. An old lady, with a cigarette in one hand and a suitcase in the other, was hurrying toward us. I closed my eyes, hoping I was seeing things, but when I opened them again she was still there. "Hi, Grandma," I said.

She ignored me. "What are you doing to my grand-daughter?" she said to Marty, who quivered and bent beneath her rage like a willow in a hailstorm. A weeping willow.

"Grandma," I said.

"Get away with you!" she said, making shooing gestures, with both hands. "Go on, ham it! She has nothing for you!"

Marty sniffed and wiped his eyes on his sleeve. He turned and would have slunk off if I hadn't grabbed him by the shoulder.

"Come back, Marty," I said.

"Go on," said Grandma.

"Back," I said. Marty, the human pinball. I stepped between him and Grandma.

"Let me explain," I said. "Quickly, before Dad gets here. Marty isn't doing anything to me. I'm doing something for him. He wants to get to Schenectady," I said.

"No, I don't dare. They don't want to see me . . ."

89

I kept my eyes on Grandma. "There is a memorial service for his brother there this afternoon. Marty hasn't seen his family in a long time. And I, um, promised him that we'd give him a lift."

"He doesn't want to come, Jane. Why not leave him here, where you found him?"

"I found him yesterday."

She stopped in the middle of a puff on her cigarette while she worked out the implications of what I'd told her, and then choked on the mouthful of smoke she probably didn't know she had.

"Do you mean," she gasped, "that this . . . Marty, has been in the van since yesterday?"

"Yesterday morning. I smuggled him aboard. Only now he's afraid to go on. Poor man."

"I'm no good," he muttered.

"So I don't know what to do," I said.

Very deliberately, Grandma dropped the cigarette and stepped on the burning butt. "You'd better tell me everything," she said grimly.

I took a deep breath, and the whole story came out in a rush. I was worried about telling it, but I felt relieved, too.

Marty didn't move, except to sway back and forth very slowly. His eyes closed. Grandma's expression as she listened was hard to read. Was she . . . could she be . . . sympathetic? Did she think I was doing a good thing? Was she going to be . . . on my side?

"Please help us, Grandma," I said.

"Stowaway!" she muttered. "Stowaway, indeed. Jane Peeler, if you were my daughter, I'd give you something to stow away and remember for a few days. Every time you sat down, you'd remember."

Oh, no. This didn't sound like sympathy.

"What will your father say? He'll have a fit!" she went on.

"But he doesn't know."

"No. No, he doesn't." Her mouth curved in a momentary smile. Then she went back to being upset with me. "What an incredibly rash and thoughtless thing to do!" she said. "You put yourself, and everyone else in the van, in danger."

"From Marty?" I mean, *really*. He weighed less than I did. "He wanted my help," I said. "And I could help him."

"You deluded girl! He's a wreck!" She shook her head. "You remind me so much of your mother. She was always one for bringing home stray animals."

Like a shaft of sunlight on a cloudy day, like the first sip of hot cocoa after a freezing skating party, like fire from heaven, a feeling of warmth went through me when I heard these words. Just like Mom. "Thank you, Grandma," I said.

"Eh? For what?"

"For giving me . . . courage. Now I know I am doing the right thing. It's what Mom would have done."

"But," she pointed at him, "he's a disgrace, a vagrant, a street person, a . . . Marty!"

I thought hard. I wanted to put this the right way. "Think of all the Martys without homes to go to," I said. "We can't help them, but we can help this one Marty. Look, Grandma. You're the one who talks about how lonely you are, how you don't matter to anyone. How no one cares what you think. Well, here's an opportunity for you. We need you. Marty needs you. Come on, Grandma. Help us get Marty home."

She didn't speak for a while. I wasn't looking at her, so I don't know if she was frowning or blushing or gnashing her teeth or what. "Is the family expecting you at the service?" she asked Marty.

I was encouraged. She was speaking directly to him.

"No," he said. "They don't care about me. Why should they?"

"Yes, they do," I said. "They wrote about you in the paper." I reached into yesterday's pocket for the tattered clipping. "So, Grandma, are you going to help us?"

"I haven't decided," she said.

Marty spoke to her for the first time. "Forget it, Grandma," he said. "Forget about Marty Oberdorf. Help that is not freely given is a chain upon the heart. I would not forge such a chain." He swayed, and almost fell. He looked about as dangerous as a piece of chewed string. "I'll be on my way. Thanks, Jane."

I didn't say anything. He staggered off.

"Wait." A cross-grained person, my grandmother.

Now that he wanted to leave, she told him to stay. He turned. "You called me Grandma. I'm not old enough to be your grandma," she said. He kept going.

"My name is Helen," she said.

Now he turned, with the smile I remembered from yesterday. The good smile. Grandma didn't swoon or anything, but she softened, the way ice cream will soften in sunshine.

"Jane, let me read that newspaper piece."

In giving the clipping to Grandma, I somehow felt as if the great burden of responsibility for Marty was being spread between us. We were together in this now. Me and Grandma, who'd have thought it? And I was happy to have her.

"Awooo! Awooo! Jane, Jane! Where are you?" Bill's voice.

Grandma moved calmly, pushing Marty into the van, putting her suitcase on top of him. "Sh," she said, putting a hand on his arm. We closed the rear door together.

"Grandma's coming!" cried Bill, "And she's. . . ."

He saw us, and stopped.

"She's already here," said Grandma. "The van's all packed. Where's your father?"

"Upstairs, with Bernie."

"Good. Run up and tell him everything's ready to go. Jane and I will be along in a moment to take a last look around the room."

He opened his mouth to say, "Yes, boss lady," thought better of it, turned and ran off.

"Thanks, Grandma," I whispered.

"Uh huh."

"You know, I don't like lying to Dad," I said.

She smiled so widely, I saw silver at the back of her mouth. I didn't know it was there.

"Are you going to tell Dad?" I asked.

"Shell, no," she said.

I nodded. It was a complicated path I'd chosen, but at least I wasn't alone on it anymore. "And do you think we can get to Schenectady in time for the service?"

"You're the one with the map, missy. You tell me."

Bill had a Danish in his mouth when we got back upstairs. There was one more left on the plate. "Would you like it?" I asked Grandma.

"Why, thank you, Jane. I believe I would." She took the last one. *Shoot.* I'd been hoping to eat it myself.

11

Gesundheit

"I think I'll sit in the backseat today," said Grandma, climbing into the van.

"Are you sure, Mother-in-law? You don't have to."

"I want to."

Bill stared at her and then at me. "But . . ." he said.

"It's okay," I whispered. "She knows. She's on our side."

He frowned. "Grandma? Grandma on our side?"

I nodded. "She's okay. I think."

Grandma was already sitting down, with her seat belt on, looking composed.

"Are you kids getting in or not?" said Dad. He was buckling Bernie's seat belt.

"I get the front seat," I said quickly.

"Do not," said Bill.

"Do so."

You know how that argument ends. Dad told us both to be quiet, and we flipped a coin to see who would sit

95

in the front seat, and I won. Bill stuck out his tongue at me, and I carefully did not stick mine out at him. I just smiled.

"Dad, Jane is teasing me," said Bill.

I buckled my seat belt and smiled at Dad. "Let's go," I said.

"Would you like some bun?" Bernie asked Bill.

"Where did you get it?" asked Bill.

"From my hand," said Bernie.

"No," said Bill.

From Watertown we drove east, toward the sun. Dad put down the sunshade on his side of the car. My sunshade was already down, so I could use the mirror on the back. When the road turned, Dad put up his sunshade. I checked my hair again. Did the color really suit me?

"It's still there," said Dad.

"What?" I asked innocently.

"That smell. I thought it was just my shirt. Don't any of you smell it?"

"I don't smell anything," said Grandma.

I turned around and caught her eye. She winked. She really did.

Bill saw her. "I don't smell anything either," he said.

"I don't smell anything from up here in the *front seat*," I said.

"Hey!" said Bill. He kicked the back of my seat.

"Maybe it's a farm you smell, Alexander," said Grandma to Dad. We were driving through countryside, but the farms were far away from the road, and all you could see was waving grass.

"I'm hungry," said Bill.

"Have a bun," said Bernie.

"Not for a bun," said Bill.

In the middle of a long, quiet stretch of road, with the windows open because of the smell, someone behind me sneezed. Not Bernie or Bill. Didn't sound like Grandma either.

"Gesundheit," said Bernie. He just learned the word a while ago. He smiled proudly. I whipped my head around. Marty sneezed again.

"Gesundheit," said Bernie.

Dad peered into the rearview mirror. "What's going on back there?" he demanded.

"Nothing," said Grandma, sticking out her chin.

"Nothing," said Bill.

"I don't know," said Bernie.

"It's about two and . . . a half hours to Schenectady," I said.

"To where?"

"Schenectady," I said. "Schenectady."

"Gesundheit," said Bernie. He thought I was sneezing.

"You mean Syracuse," said Dad. The signs at the side of the road said SYRACUSE.

"Do I?"

We caught up to a slow-moving pickup truck. We hung behind it while a couple of cars zipped past in the other direction. Then Dad pulled out to pass the truck. A noisy and dilapidated vehicle, it belched deep blue smoke out of its exhaust pipe. The tailgate banged up and down. Green paint flaked off the sides. The driver's door was held shut with string. An old truck driven by an old man with a hat on. I waved and smiled at him as we passed. He didn't wave back. Big thick glasses on his face and, underneath them, a frown full of yellow teeth. The hands gripping the wheel were enormous.

He sped up, keeping pace with us. Dad sped up some more, and so did the old man with the thick glasses. The truck made loud complaining noises, but kept even with us. We were in the oncoming lane. Fortunately, no cars were oncoming.

Dad honked the horn and pointed. The old man shook his head. He didn't want us to pass. A mean old man. "What the . . ." Dad began.

In the distance I could see a car coming toward us. Dad sighed and slowed down, to get in behind the truck again – and then the mean old man slowed down. We were stuck beside his dirty old truck, with a car coming right at us. The old man glared. Did he want us to get hurt? Dad put his driving foot to the floor. The truck started to speed up, too, then backfired noisily and slowed enough for us to get in front of it. Seconds later the oncoming car passed us. Dad kept his foot to the floor. The truck disappeared behind us.

"I think I need a new diaper," said Bernie.

"Me, too," said Dad.

"I'm sorry," said Bernie. "I forgot to tell you."

"Next time," said Dad. "Tell us next time."

"Are we there yet?" said Bill. "I'm hungry."

"Do you want to stop for a snack?" asked Dad.

"No, let's not stop," I said. I had the map out on my knee, and a pad of paper. I was figuring out how much farther we had to go. I didn't want to stop. It was ten thirty and we were still a long way from Schenectady. If we were going to get Marty to the church on time, we couldn't afford to stop for long. And, of course, the longer we took to Schenectady, the longer it would be before we got to Auntie Vera's.

"But Bill's hungry," said Dad. "I've seen a couple of fruit stands. Fresh blueberries. I wouldn't mind a rest. I didn't get much sleep last night."

"Oh, let's not stop yet," said Grandma.

"I thought you might want to . . ."

"I can wait awhile longer."

"And Bill can have something to eat," I said, "right here. Have a mint, Bill."

"Have a banana, Hannah," sang Dad. "Have some baloney, Tony. Have some chili, Billy." My Dad likes old songs. We were all named for songs he likes.

"Have a mint, Clint. Have a candy, Andy." Dad was making up verses now. "Have a peanut, I mean it. 'Cause . . ."

"Everybody eats when they come to my house," sang – someone. That's the next line. Bill knew the song; Dad sings it a lot. But it wasn't Bill's voice. And it wasn't Grandma's.

"Quiet, down there!" said Grandma.

"I didn't say anything," said Bill and Bernie together.

"I wasn't talking to you," said Grandma.

"There's our turnoff," I said. "Next stop, Rome."

We turned left, which brought the sun into my eyes. We drove a little longer. When we came to a big fruit stand that advertised REAL CHEAP BERRIES, Dad pulled over.

I offered to change Bernie, to save time. "Buy your fruit," I said. "I'll wait in the car."

Grandma got a cigarette going right away.

Dad was back very quickly. "These aren't great prices," he said. "The berries were cheaper back in Pulaski."

For a horrible moment I thought he wanted to turn back, which would have thrown off the whole schedule. "Let's get going then," said Grandma. She butted out her cigarette, even though she wasn't finished. Dad offered again to let her smoke in the van.

She shook her head and ground out the butt before climbing back into the rear seat. "It's a stupid habit. I know I'm poisoning myself, but I don't want anyone else on my conscience."

"You see," I whispered to Bill. "She cares about us. She's not so bad."

"She looks the same to me," he said.

The next stretch of our journey passed quickly, though not quickly enough for me. Between the picturesque little cities and towns, the landscape was green and rich and pleasant to look at, full of dotty little farms and silos, each worth a point. The sun shone; the wheat waved; the signs in front of the gas stations spun bravely, advertising bigger and better and cheaper. We passed Rome and Utica and a bunch of little places. The Mohawk River ran smoothly beside us. Everything looked fresh, as though it had just come from the store. Hills, streets, mailboxes, front porches, sheep – they all had crisp edges and stood well against the backdrop of fields and sky.

"We're making pretty good time," said Dad.

"Still . . . almost two thumbs to go," I said. "That's over two hours."

"Do you think, Alexander," Grandma asked hesitantly, "that we might have time to make a tiny detour to Schenectady, on our way to Pittsfield?"

"Schenectady?" said Dad. He turned quickly to dart a look at me. "Jane mentioned Schenectady earlier. What is it about that place?"

"Oh, nothing much." Grandma was elaborately casual. "I think they have a museum. And some old churches. And a baseball team. And, maybe, a few nice restaurants."

"I guess we could stop there for a bit," I said.

Dad stared at me. "You didn't want to stop for blueberries."

What could I tell him? "I don't really like blueberries."

"I'd like to see . . . Schenectady," said Bill, relishing the word. The way he said it, it sounded like someone ripping paper in half. "A whole new planet to explore!" The planet of the Oberdorfs.

"Are you serious, Bill? Do you want to go to Schenectady, too?" said Dad.

"Wilco! Maybe we'll get to see a dead guy."

"Bill!" Grandma and I said together.

The tires were saying *Popocatepetl, Popocatepetl, Popocatepetl,* as they bumped along a poorly paved stretch of road. And then the van made an unhappy noise, something between a grind and a groan. We slowed down. Steam started to leak from under the hood. Dad steered to the side of the narrow highway – it was only two lanes wide, and looked like a country road – and let the van come to a complete halt. The tires were silent now. With the engine shut off, I could hear the tick of cooling metal, and the hiss of escaping steam.

12

Good Fairy

We sat at the side of the road. No cars passed. The landscape was deserted. Trees overhung this section of road. I looked at the map on my knee and felt sick.

"Anyone want a mint?" said Dad.

"Well," said Grandma. "Aren't you going to get out and open the hood?" She sounded a bit snippy. More worried than angry, though.

I was beyond anger, beyond worry. I felt hopeless.

Steam poured out from the front of the van, as if there were a little witch's cauldron underneath the hood. Dad turned around in his seat. "Why would I do that?"

"To fix the engine, of course."

Dad smiled. "But, Mother-in-law, I don't know how to fix it."

She made a noise of exasperation. *Tchah*, it sounded like.

"Sorry. I wish there was a way to fix the van. I wish that a good fairy would suddenly pop out of the backseat and announce an intimate knowledge of the internal combustion engine."

"Aren't you even going to check under the hood?"

"No," he said.

"Tchah!" she said again.

"Gesundheit," said Bernie.

Dad turned around and started to cough. His eyes opened wide and he pointed, like the heroine's girl-friend in the horror movie just before the "Thing" gets her. I turned around to see what had panicked my father, and saw a long skinny arm reaching over the back of the rear seat. A skinny arm, with a skinny hand attached. A not-quite-clean hand, a man's hand, though the nails were rather long. Marty's hand.

After a moment, Marty's head appeared over the back of the seat.

"Are you okay, Dad?" I asked.

He nodded. "Swallowed my mint," he whispered.

Grandma helped Marty climb over the backseat, and sit beside her. The smell was stronger. "Bit dusty back there," he said. "Cramped, too. Hello, Jane. Helen."

Dad glared at me. I blushed.

Bernie couldn't see over the back of his car seat. "Who is there?" he asked.

"A man named Marty," I told him. "He's a stow-away."

Bernie digested this for a moment. Dad didn't speak.

"Do you know him?" Bernie asked me.

"I don't," Bill put in hurriedly. *Coward.* "Not really."

"Yes," I said. "So do Grandma and Bill."

"Oh. That's okay, then," Bernie said.

I was glad to have Bernie's approval. I was more worried about Dad. He hadn't gone this long without saying anything since last spring, when he had laryngitis.

Marty spoke first. "Well, I guess you'll want me to take a look under the hood. Would you mind opening it? Please," he added.

"Who are you?" Dad croaked. "What are you doing here? What's going on? WOULD SOMEONE TELL ME WHAT IS GOING ON?"

My spirits sank as Dad's voice rose higher. "It was all my fault," I began.

"No, it was my responsibility, dear." Grandma had a soft little smile that actually looked like it belonged on her face. "Alexander, if you're going to waste time getting angry, you might as well get angry at me."

"How do you know," said Dad, "that I'm going to get mad? Why would I get mad that you two smuggled a strange man into our family van without telling me? Who would get mad at being circumvented, manipulated, and lied to?"

Oh, dear. His eyebrows jumped up and down as he talked. They looked like a pair of fighting caterpillars.

Grandma tried to speak, but I stopped her. "Dad, do you remember when I told you about punching the bully in grade three?"

"No," said Dad, eyebrows down, frowning.

"I do," said Bill.

"It was like punching the bully. We had a long talk and you told me that there were some things that were sort of wrong and sort of right at the same time. Greg the bully, remember? He used to take our cookies? And I punched him in the nose when I was wearing my Hercules ring of power, and he bled all over the place, and I got sent to the principal's office?"

"Oh, yes, of course." Eyebrows up almost to his hairline.

"And you made me write an apology to Greg, and then you gave me seconds at dessert?"

"Yes."

"Well, it was like that with Marty. Taking him with us was wrong, and it was right, too. It was. I asked Mom about it last night."

A car went past us going the other way.

Dad's jaw fell open like a trapdoor. "Your mother knows?" he said.

"Sort of."

"Are you going to fix this van or not?" Grandma was sounding testy.

"I am not," said Dad.

"What kind of –"

"Now, Helen," Marty spoke up. "Not everyone can fix cars." Sitting next to her on the backseat, his head came up to just past her shoulder. The expression on his face was reproving. "If you beat a cow, it will not lay eggs for you."

Bill snickered.

Dad scowled. "If you think I'm about to –"

"Dad, please, we're falling behind. It might be simple."

"It would have to be pretty darned simple for me to be able to do anything about it. I'm not bad at fixing kids' toys, or changing lightbulbs, but that's my limit. If there's a broken *lego* carburetor in there, maybe I'd be able to rebuild it. And even then, I'd need the instruction booklet."

"There is no carburetor in this van," said Marty. "It has fuel injection."

Of course, he knew about engines. I remembered him talking about ours this morning. Hope flew up inside me like a startled bird.

"Dad, you have to let Marty try." I could picture Mom all by herself at *The Music Man*.

"Do you know how to fix cars?" asked Dad.

Marty ducked his head. "It is why I climbed out of the storage area. Didn't you say you wanted someone to come and fix the car? A good fairy? I thought I heard you say that."

Dad stared at him. "I believe I did say that."

"And so I thought, Marty, here is something you can do."

"So you are the good fairy I called into being? You can fix our van?"

"I can try," he said, "to repay you for your kindness in taking me to . . ."

"Schenectady?" Dad finished the sentence for him.

I don't know about Grandma, but I felt guilty.

"How," Bernie asked, "can something be wrong and right at the same time?"

Dad sighed. "Don't you start. I heard about that from your mom for days."

Dad handed me a bag of jelly beans and told me to take the boys to look at the cows in the pasture while Marty looked at the van. "Bernie, don't wander away," he said. Bernie nodded solemnly. "And Bill, don't climb over the fence." Bill's shoulders slumped.

We hopped across a dry ditch, except for Bernie, who hopped through it, and climbed up the bank to the pasture. We looked at the cows and ate jelly beans. "No black ones, Bernie," I said. "They're not good for you."

"Oh," he said.

Bill and I ate the black ones.

"Have you noticed his fingernails?" Bill asked me, his mouth full.

"Marty's?"

"No, Grandma's. Of course, Marty's. They're like claws."

Yes, I'd noticed. "Maybe he's a vampire," I said.

"Yes. He is from Schenectady after all. Maybe he's a werewolf."

We were joking, but Bernie started to whimper. I felt bad. "Sorry, little guy," I said. "Here, have a black jelly bean. They're really tasty."

He whimpered some more. "But they're bad for you."

O what a tangled web we weave. "Okay," I said, and ate the black jelly bean.

We were standing in the shade of a pine tree. Near us

was a farm fence – strands of rusty wire strung between thick, old posts. On the other side of the fence stood the inhabitants of the field: huge, ungainly, piebald beasts, large-eyed, deep-voiced, uncaring. Bill regarded them with a thoughtful eye.

"Alien life-forms," he said. "They should be investigated."

"They are cows," said Bernie.

"They have horns, Bernie. Horns. And they have four stomachs." Bill made his voice sound low and thrilling – as low and thrilling as a ten-year-old can. "Think of that, Bernie. Pretty strange, hey?"

Bernie nodded.

"Fortunately, I am fluent in the cow language. Let me see if I can communicate with them." Bill went up against the fence and mooed as loudly as he could.

The cows looked up.

"Ah, ha! Contact!" he said. "Now I'll ask them to take me to their leader." He mooed again. And, very slowly, the cows began to amble over.

Bill put his hand on a strand of wire.

"Remember what Dad said," I told him.

"What?" he called over his shoulder, without looking back. "What business is it of yours, Miss Bossy?"

"Bill, you're going to get in trouble for nothing." I clenched my fists in frustration. We were falling behind schedule. Everything was being pushed back – Schenectady, the Berkshires, *The Music Man*.

"Nothing?" said Bill. "Communication with aliens is not nothing."

"Climbing a stupid fence is nothing. Dad is already upset about Marty. Come on, Bill. Don't make it harder on him."

He pulled himself up higher. Now his head was level with the top of the fence. "He's not upset with *me* about Marty," he said.

"Why," Bernie asked, his big eyes on me, his throat sliding up and down as he swallowed a jelly bean, "is Dad upset about Marty?"

Bill stuck his foot into a twisted clump of wire, and pulled himself up to the top of the fence. "Moooooo," he called.

"Marty is a stowaway. Remember? Do you know what a stowaway is?"

Bernie frowned. "Is it a vegetable?"

"No. It's someone who hides in your van, and you don't know he's there."

Bernie nodded to himself.

Bill's foot was caught in the tangle of wire. He wiggled his foot, but it wouldn't come free. He couldn't climb up, and he couldn't climb down.

"Hey, Jane," said Bill.

"Yes?"

"Uh. Help." He wiggled his foot harder.

"Help with what?"

"Come on, Jane. Get me down."

I like Bill. I really do. But I couldn't help myself. I didn't move.

"Jane, please!" Bill hung on with one hand while he tried to free his foot with the other. He sounded scared. I figured enough was enough, and moved forward to help him.

"BILL! BILL PEELER! GET DOWN!"

"Oh, shoot," he said.

13

Good Comes from Evil

"GET DOWN FROM THAT FENCE!" Dad roared.

"Hang on, Bill." I pulled the shoe off his foot, which, of course, he hadn't thought to try to do. With his foot free he climbed down easily, but the shoe remained stuck at eye level. I set about untying it. I've always been pretty good at knots.

Dad came bounding toward us, still roaring. He sounded like a hungry lion. Bill bowed his head, a one-sandaled Christian resigned to his fate.

"What did I say?" Dad shouted. "What did I tell you not to do?"

"Climb the fence," Bill mumbled.

"And what did you do?"

"Climb the fence."

"That's the second time in two days! What am I going to do with you?"

What do they call those questions where you aren't supposed to answer? Not categorical, but something like that. Stupid is what they are, but there's another

word. Anyway, Dad's question was one of those. Bill knew better than to try and answer it. Silently, I handed him his shoe, and he bent down to put it on.

"I can't send you to your room because we're in the van. I can't yell at you for the next hour because I'd get hoarse. What am I going to do?"

Another trick question. Bill didn't look up. Bernie was frowning.

Dad sighed. "Let's get back to the van."

We trooped back. I offered Bill the bag of jelly beans. He shook his head.

Marty was sitting on the step of the van. He looked tired. He took a whole handful of jelly beans.

"I have discovered the trouble," he said.

"What is it?" said Dad. Standing beside the little old man, he looked like a giant.

"I wonder," said Marty, looking around, "if there is

any water around here? Did you see any water when you were up by the field, Jane?"

"No," I said.

"That's too bad," said Marty.

"There is water," said Bill. "A little stream on the other side of the fence. It's hidden from the road. The cows told me about it," he added, in a low voice.

"Ah, ha!" Marty stood up. "There is a stream beyond the fence," he said. It sounded like one of those phrases I had to learn in French class. *Il y a un ruisseau au delà de la clôture.* The hairs of my aunt are shorter than those of my mama. My car has a pain in the gas tank.

I wondered what Marty was getting at. He looked earnest, like he was trying to be helpful, but what he said didn't sound helpful.

Dad frowned. "Thank you. There is a stream beyond the fence. And there are clouds in the sky. In the nearby copse, a lonesome red-winged blackbird sings its song of love. Thank you for the nature lesson. Now could you tell us what's wrong with the van?"

"There is water in the stream," continued Marty.

"And a bump on the log, and the green grass grows all around all around. Come on, Marty." Dad was getting impatient. I think he was upset that he couldn't fix the car, even if it was something simple.

"I wonder if there is a can in the car," said Marty. "An empty can. Or a bottle. Or a hat."

"A hat?" I asked.

"A hat for water."

"What's a hat for water?" Was it another obscure figure of speech, like the one about the cow and the eggs?

Marty made a gesture with his hands. "You put the water from the stream into the radiator of the car."

"Oh," said Dad.

"And the radiator would cool down the car. Now the radiator is not working, and the car is too hot."

"Oh," said Dad again. "And we could carry the water in a can. If we had a can. Or a bottle. If we had a bottle."

"Yes. Or a hat," I said.

"If we had a hat," said Bill.

Dad and Bill went back up the hill to find the stream. Grandma lit a cigarette. Bernie and I got down on our hands and knees to root around the floor of the van and through our vacation luggage. Bernie found an old waxed paper cup, which used to have a milkshake inside it, and now had a dried butterscotch crust. I found five baseball caps, with holes all over them for ventilation, and a couple of twist ties. Bernie found a pen and a peppermint lifesaver. I found thirteen cents.

Dad came around to the side door. "The stream is there all right. We'll be able to get all the water we need. What did you guys find?" We showed the results of our search. His face fell. "That's it? That's all you found? Did you check our beach stuff? What about plastic buckets?"

"We have shovels," said Bernie. "And rakes."

"No buckets?"

"No buckets."

Dad took the dixie cup from Bernie's hand. Stared at it doubtfully.

It was a glorious day, if a little buggy, on our secluded little patch of highway. Dad stared from the cup to the farmer's fence. Bill stood on the other side of it, wagging his finger up and down in front of a cow's face, as if he was arguing with the animal. Grandma was butting out her cigarette.

"Are we going to wait here all day?" she said.

You can't carry a lot of water in a dixie cup with a hole in the bottom. You can't carry any water at all in a well-ventilated baseball cap. Marty suggested using plastic bags, which we should have thought of. Everyone has plastic bags in their car. Bernie and I went back and rummaged around. The first plastic bag we found had a big hole in it. So did the second plastic bag. The third bag had three holes. After that he stopped looking. I kept at it, and found a fluff-covered mint, a whole bunch of twist ties, and another seven cents.

"This is going to be a long, slow process," said Dad, after running with the dripping plastic bag in one hand, and the dripping dixie cup in the other, and finally pouring about three teaspoonfuls of water into the steaming radiator.

"A raindrop does not fill a bucket," said Marty, "but enough raindrops will fill an ocean."

The expression on Dad's face was hilarious, but I didn't feel like laughing.

Marty gestured into the engine. "There is, I think, another problem."

That's when we saw the approaching car. Ahead of us was a straight stretch of road. Dad ran into the oncoming lane and started waving his arms, stopping just in time to jump out of the way as the car sped past.

Then, from around the bend behind us, we heard the sound of another vehicle. A noisier vehicle by far – a rackety-banging, slow-moving, backfiring vehicle. The noise stopped and started and came on again, and then we saw the rusty pickup truck chugging toward us. You know how you always seem to see the same cars over and over again when you're traveling? This was the truck we'd had so much trouble passing. Blue smoke bellied out of its exhaust pipe.

Dad was careful to stay on the side of the road. He made a half-wave at the driver, who grinned a wide yellow-toothed grin. The truck crawled slowly past us, backfiring. It didn't stop. The tailgate flapped up and down, like a waving hand. When the truck hit a pothole, down the road from us, the tailgate opened and something bounced out of the truck. It fell onto the road, bounced again, and rolled. A clear bright flashing thing. The bottle – that's what it was – came to rest on the gravel edge of the road. The truck lurched slowly away into the distance, belching smelly smoke and sudden spurts of flame.

I ran to get the bottle. "It's not broken," I said, holding it up to the sun.

Marty shuddered when he saw it. "Whiskey," he said.

"Not now," said Dad.

Marty looked away.

Dad took the bottle from me, ran to the fence, passed the bottle to Bill, and came back a minute later with a bottle full of water. He poured carefully. I stood on tiptoe to watch.

Marty was on his knees at the side of the van. "Are you okay?" Grandma asked him. "Marty, are you okay?"

He nodded. Dad ran back to the fence for another bottle of water. And another. Bill came back with him the last time.

"Funny, isn't it," I said. I was thinking back to the man trying not to let us pass him, and then laughing at us as he went past us. "That mean old guy in the truck didn't like us, but the bottle fell out of his truck, and it helped us."

"Funny," Dad agreed.

"How come that is?" I asked.

"Good comes from evil sometimes," said Dad. "I don't know why. But I'm sure Marty has a saying about it."

Marty climbed to his feet, dusting off the knees of his pants. His face was as empty as Dad's bottle. "There is still a problem with the hose," he said.

"Oh," said Dad.

Marty explained. "The hose comes out of the radiator. There should be a clamp." He made a circle with his thumb and first finger. "To hold the hose. Only now there is no clamp. And the water drains out of the radiator." He pointed underneath the front of the van. A small puddle of water was forming.

"What do we do?"

"Many people carry spare clamps in their tool kits," said Marty.

Dad shook his head. "Not us. We don't even carry a tool kit."

"Then," said Marty, "we have a problem."

"Tchah," said Grandma.

Dad sighed. "Anyone want a mint?" he called. The boys jumped to their feet. I got the candy from the front seat. I caught sight of my hair in the driving mirror. It was starting to look less chestnut and more pumpkin. I pushed it behind my ears, to show off the heart earrings.

"If there was only a way to tie off the hose," said Marty.

"Like what?"

"Thin wire might work. It'd be a temporary job, but it should last for a couple of hours. Not a coat hanger, thinner than that . . ."

Dad frowned, shaking his head. By accident I bit into my mint and, like a jolt of flavor, an idea came into my head. I ran back to the van and collected the twist ties I'd found on the floor.

"Could you use these?" I asked.

Fifteen minutes later, we were ready to get back on the road.

"Thank you, Marty," we all said, one after the other. He looked away. His hands, I noticed, were trembling.

"Now, is there anything we can do for you in return?" Dad asked. "Anything you might need . . ." He stopped. Marty was climbing into the van.

"Yes," said Dad, to himself. "I suppose we could do that."

14

My Attorney, Bernie

Marty sat in the backseat beside Grandma, eating jelly beans.

"Are you old enough to eat the black ones?" Bernie asked, seriously.

"I don't really know," Marty said.

Bernie nodded. "I am almost three," he said.

Bill, in the front seat, turned around to stare at Marty. "You don't know how old you are?" he said with surprise. A grown-up who didn't know his age.

"Well, I'm older than my brother. Two years . . . I think . . . or three. I used to carry around a piece of paper with my date of birth on it," said Marty. He ran the words together, like he'd heard them a lot and thought of them as one word: date-of-birth. "But I lost it a while ago."

"You could ask your mom and dad," said Bernie.

Marty smiled sadly and shook his head. "No, I can't."

"Or your brothers and sisters. They would know."

Marty shook his head again. "I have no brothers," he said. "Not anymore."

"Why not?"

"Bernie," I said. "Shush now."

Dad drove in silence. The morning was wearing away gently, like the edge of a cliff with water at the bottom. Imperceptibly, the sun was getting higher; the day was getting older; the cliff was receding.

Dad didn't seem as angry anymore. He had forgiven Bill for climbing the fence against his express orders. Marty had said something about forbidden actions breaking the boundaries of knowledge. Bernie had said, "You know . . ." and then stopped.

We were nearing Amsterdam. The road signs mentioned Schenectady coming up. No one in the car commented on it.

Grandma and Marty were sitting together on the backseat. Not arm in arm or anything, but they were clearly getting along pretty well. I must say, I never thought I'd be doing Grandma a good turn when I smuggled Marty aboard. At the time – was it only yesterday? – I didn't much care about Grandma. But I was glad she was with us now. She was growing on me.

"You know," Bernie said, "Dad told Bill not to climb over the fence."

"So?" I said. I was sitting next to him.

"Well, Bill didn't climb *over* the fence."

"Hey," said Bill. "That's right. Not until you told me to climb over the fence."

Dad laughed.

I grabbed Bernie's hand and shook it. "You're quite the lawyer, aren't you?" I said.

From behind me, Marty said, surprisingly, "My attorney, Bernie."

"Exactly right," said Dad. "That's where he got his name. Do you know that song?"

Marty smiled. "There are many songs about the name Bernard. How about this one?" Without even clearing his throat, he sang about a wonderful guy who could do anything anyone else could do – only better:

Edward traveled wide and far, by plane and train,
    by boat and car,
But no matter where the journey,
Ed didn't go as far as – Bernie.
Megan studied long and deep, subjects that put
    most to sleep,
Still, no matter what she'd learn, she
Never got as smart as – Bernie.
Robert milked the cows and then, he made more
    cheese than fifteen men,
But quick as he could work the churn, he
Never made as much as – Bernie."

Marty had a high, clear voice. Much better than Dad's. For all the silliness of the song, the music hung in the air like a shimmering curtain. Marty wiped his eyes very theatrically, as if he was about to cry again, only he sang instead, drawing out the poignancy of the last verse:

> Jane's a lass that loved too well, a tale as sad as
>   tongue can tell,
> And yet no matter how she'd yearn, she
> Never loved as hard as – Bernie.

When he finished, we all applauded. Bernie's eyes were wide and round as soup ladles. Grandma's face was lighter than I had ever seen it. She liked hearing Marty sing. She liked the sound of his voice.

"Marty," said Dad, "I'm glad you shared that with us."

I felt myself relax. I hadn't really known how unrelaxed I was. Funny how you can be a certain way and not know it until you stop being that way. I remember really liking this boy, Armand, in my class. We'd write notes to each other and walk each other home – actually, he walked me home because he lived farther away from school than I did – and I thought it was too bad that my friend Bridget didn't like Armand as much as I did, and started playing with a different group of girls instead of with me. I was happy, but I didn't know it until Armand stopped writing notes to me and started writing them to Bridget instead. She wrote him back, and it turned out that she'd liked him all along. I was miserable for days and days. Then Armand put a cut-in-half worm into one of Bridget's notes, and laughed when she screamed. And I realized the kind of boy he was.

Anyway, the point was that Marty was part of the trip now. Dad accepted him. And that made us all feel better.

"Marty, where do you want to go in Schenectady?"

"To the Episcopalian church on the square," said Marty. "It is easy to find."

"And when does the service start?"

Marty didn't answer.

"Two o'clock," I said. In an hour and a half.

"Marty," said Bill, "are you older than Dad?"

"Oh, yes. I am older than everyone."

"You're not older than I am," said Grandma. "We both remember a lot of the same things."

"But you look so young, Helen," he said.

And Helen – I mean Grandma – looked away with a shy smile.

There was a lot I wanted to ask Marty, but I didn't know how to go about it. Did he have a wife, or children? Why didn't he have enough money for bus fare? I decided the questions were too personal. I didn't want to upset him, or Dad.

Bernie had questions, too. "Are you a monster?" he asked Marty.

"A monster?" Maybe Marty thought he had heard wrong.

"You have claws, you know."

"Bernard!" said Grandma.

But Marty laughed and held up his hands. "Notice, Bernie, how one hand has long nails, but the other does not." I must say, all his nails looked pretty long to me – long for a man anyway. But they were really hanging off of one hand.

"When you play the guitar, you need long nails to pluck the strings," he explained.

"You play the guitar?" I said.

He smiled. His gums had worn away like the morning, and his teeth stuck a long way out. They looked as long as his nails, and there were about the same number of them. "I have been all around with my guitar. I used to have my own band. One year I drove a broken-down bus full of musicians all over North America. That's where I learned how to fix engines."

"What happened to your guitar?" Bill asked.

"I lost it."

"And you're not a monster?" said Bernie.

"No," he said.

"Good," said Bernie.

15

Old-People Talk

Amsterdam, New York is great city to have lunch in. I
know, because we had a great lunch there. The van was
in a gas station getting the radiator put right, and we
were in a restaurant that served everything with a huge
plate of chunky french fries. Some of the fries were
bigger than Bernie's hand.

"Let's pretend to be food," said Bill. "I'm a huge
strong french fry," he said, waving one around.

"Child," I said. Dad was in the bathroom and I was
the oldest one at the table.

I checked my watch: one fifteen. The van was going
to be ready at one thirty.

"I'm another french fry," said Bernie.

"No, you have to pick something different," Bill pro-
tested. "I'm a french fry – you can be a chicken nugget.
Or a corned beef sandwich." That's what Dad was having.

"Ugh!" we all said.

"Okay. I'm Mona the milkshake," I said. We were all
drinking them. The menu said they were famous, and I

could believe it. I was almost finished mine. "Mmm," I said.

"Can I be another milkshake?" Bernie asked me.

"Sure," I said. "You can be chocolate and I'll be vanilla."

"I am walking across the plate to see what I can conquer," said Bill. "And what is this I see? A chocolate milkshake, all unprepared for my attack!" He held a french fry in his hand like an action figure, and jumped it across the table.

Dad came back then. "I called Mom to tell her we'd be a bit late," he said, sitting down. "She's made a dinner reservation for the two of you for five thirty."

"Great," I said.

Grandma and Marty weren't with us. Neither of them had wanted lunch. They were off somewhere in the city, doing some shopping. That's what Grandma said anyway, as she dragged Marty away. He wasn't up to saying much.

"Do you think Marty misses his brother?" I asked Dad. "I wonder how it feels when your brother dies?"

"Hey!" said Bernie, clutching at his container and, of course, knocking it over. Bernie's a slow drinker, and there was still a fair amount of milkshake left. Only now, of course, there wasn't. There was, however, a fair amount of milkshake on the table, and on his french fries, and on Dad's corned beef sandwich.

Dad shouted. For a moment I was afraid I'd find out how it felt when your brother dies.

Dad used up all our napkins and some from the empty table next to us, and Bernie cried over the spilt milkshake, and Bill smirked until Dad told him to share his lunch with Bernie, and I sat very still in my chair, thankful that, for once, I had eaten quickly.

Lunch continued. I checked my wrist – one twenty-five.

I saw Grandma and Marty first. My first thought was, *He's changed his clothes*. Then I remembered he didn't bring any. He was wearing a neat dark suit and a shirt and tie. He'd had a haircut and his face was shaved, all except for a little mustache I hadn't noticed on his unshaven face. And his shoes were different.

Grandma looked the same. No, that's not quite true. She looked the same, but different from inside. I don't know how to explain it. It was as if a process of trans-formation, begun back when she first saw Marty, had gone forward another step. She was another degree less like the Grandma I used to know, and more like some other, better person. She looked happier. Maybe that's what I mean.

Anyway, she and Marty came over to our sticky, napkin-covered table, and she smiled at us. "Had an accident?"

"It was Bernie," Bill began.

"Bill started it," Bernie said.

And Grandma kept smiling. Pretty good smile, too.

"You look like you're going to a wedding," I told Marty.

He didn't look happy, like Grandma. He looked nervous. And he didn't smell musty anymore. He smelled funny, though. "Not a wedding," he said.

No, of course; it was a memorial service.

"What is that smell?" asked Bernie. Not often he gets to ask that one. Usually someone else asks it about him.

Grandma smiled. "Mothballs," she said.

"What are mothballs?" Bill asked. "I've never smelled them before."

Grandma smiled. "Imagine never having heard of mothballs."

"Imagine," I said, just to make Bill mad.

"I remember a trunk in my uncle's room, growing up," said Marty. "He used to live with us, my mother's brother. He kept his best clothes in that trunk, and on special Friday nights he would get dressed up and go out. I remember the smell on his clothes as he walked down the hall. When I got my first suit, I hung it up with mothballs in the pockets, and when I put it on, I smelled just like my uncle. I felt so grown-up."

Grandma listened with a "me, too" expression on her face. "I wore my grandmother's fur wrap to my senior year dance," she said. "And the smell of the mothballs was so strong that the whole cloakroom simply reeked for days. Oh, my, what a fuss!" She sniffed, thinking back.

The waitress had cleared everything away. Now she came back to stand beside the table wearing a very wait-ressly expression: not "me, too," more like "so what?"

Dad gestured to Grandma and Marty. "Do you want some lunch? You ought to have something to eat, apart from jelly beans. What about you, Mother-in-law?"

"We had a hot dog in the street," she said. "On our way to the used-clothing store."

"Do you want anything else? Something to drink? Dessert? Coffee?"

"I'm not thirsty," said Marty quickly. "Or hungry."

"We should be on our way," said Grandma.

I checked my watch – one thirty. "The van will be ready now," I said.

Dad nodded. "Okay, then. Just the check, please."

"Sure," said the waitress.

Grandma and Marty sat next to each other again. The mothball smell was noticeable. Not really horrible, but kind of sharp. We decided to keep the windows open. The wind racketed around, so it was hard to hear what everyone else was saying. Bernie and Bill were sitting beside each other in the middle seat, pretending to be supersonic jets. Every now and then I could hear Grandma saying, "And remember . . ." and Marty saying, "In New York, we already had . . ." whatever it was. Ice trucks, I think, which didn't make any sense.

"Why have a truck for ice when you can make it in the freezer?" I asked Dad. I was in the front.

"When Marty and Grandma were little, there weren't any freezers."

"Oh."

"It's old-people talk," he said.

"The way you and Mom go on about having to walk all the way across the living room just to change channels on the TV?"

"Yes. Like that. Your grandmother doesn't have too many people her age to talk to."

"Dad," I whispered, "what's a mothball?"

He smiled sideways at me. "I thought you knew."

We were on a real highway now. Big trucks all around us. By the side of the road, I could see factories and, every now and again, the river. It was wide here – a stretch of flat, brown water, crossed by metal bridges that lifted in the middle so that boats could go through.

The big green sign wiggled in the wind.

"Schenectady!" cried Bill, as we drove underneath it. "Attention, aliens of Schenectady, we have landed!"

"Take the first turnoff," called Marty from the backseat. His voice wavered.

Dad angled the van across the road without slowing down. Someone behind us honked. Dad waved.

Schenectady needs someone to pave its roads. I thought it was the drivers who were weird, skewing all over the road and bumping up and down, but it's the potholes. We were doing it, too – bumping across potholes, steering around potholes, just missing other cars doing the same thing. "Whizz! Bang! Boom!" shouted Bill.

"Turn . . . let me see . . . turn right at the next light," said Marty. "Then follow the signs for downtown."

"Don't worry," said Grandma, patting his arm. "It'll be okay."

"What'll I say?" asked Marty. "What'll I tell them?"

"Don't worry," said Grandma again.

"I don't know if I can do it."

Downtown turned out to be a square with a park in the middle, and a statue surrounded by cannons and benches and people eating ice cream. Around the square were big government buildings, and banks, and a church. Marty peered at the church.

"We're too early," he said.

"No, we're not." Grandma spoke soothingly. I checked. Ten to two. *Perfect.*

Dad pulled the van onto a side street and parked. "Here you are, Marty. Good luck."

"Thank you for the ride," said Marty faintly. He didn't move.

"Marty," said Grandma, "would you like our help? Would it be easier for you if all of us came with you to the memorial service?"

"Would you?" His face brightened three shades. He looked like a condemned prisoner with a reprieve.

"Of course we would," said Grandma.

"Wait a minute," said Dad. "We can't just barge in on a strange family gathering. We're not dressed for it. We couldn't –"

"We'd be honored," said Grandma.

"I want to go, too," said Bill.

"And I want . . ." I paused. I didn't know what I wanted. On the one hand, I wanted to see Mom. We were less than two hours from Pittsfield. We could be at Auntie Vera's by four o'clock. Only a few hours off my original estimate. On the other hand, I wanted to see Marty's homecoming. The way to Schenectady had been long and twisted and, to a large extent, it had been my choosing. I wanted to see the end of the journey.

"I want to be a big boy," said Bernie.

Dad turned to stare at him. "Now?"

"Right now."

16

Where's Marty?

Dad reached for the diaper bag.

"No," said Bernie. "I don't need a new diaper. I want to be a big boy."

Dad tensed, suddenly alert, the way a hunter tenses when, after a long night's wait by the water hole, the tiger finally slinks into view.

"You want to use a bathroom?" he asked, his eyes ranging up and down the side street. A coin laundry; a place that fixed computers; a place that fixed vacuum cleaners; an auto repair shop. Lots of broken things in Schenectady, apparently. No restaurant, or hotel, or public library. No place with bathrooms. And then, down the street at the corner, beckoning invitingly – the church.

Bernie nodded. On his face was a look of inward concentration. "Big boy," he whispered.

Dad jumped out of the car, ran around, pulled Bernie out of the car seat, and bent over his backside to give him that very embarrassing parental check. "You're clean," he said. "Okay, everyone. We're going to the church. Bill, Jane, you stay with me. Mother-in-law, we'll meet you and Marty inside as soon as we can."

We hurried. Dad, carrying Bernie in his arms, the diaper bag swinging from his shoulder, set a tough pace. I didn't look back to see how Grandma and Marty were doing.

There were police in front of the church. Also a couple who looked like funeral people: striped pants, long gray suit jackets, very clean faces. They were putting up NO PARKING signs. They do that at the churches near our house, too.

Dad hurried up the steps. We followed.

There was a man inside the doors, with a sad expression on his face. He came toward us right away. "I'm so sorry for your loss," he said, when he got up to us. I guess we must have looked very agitated.

"Actually," said Dad, "I don't want to, um, intrude, but I was wondering if there was a place we could . . . my little boy here . . ."

"Oh. Yes, of course, sir. This way."

He led us down the aisle of the church. I like the way churches smell – musty and full of memories. This was an old church, but even new churches smell like that. When my friend Bridget got confirmed, there was a party for all the confirmed people and their parents and friends downstairs afterward, and even the party room smelled very nice.

The sad-looking man led us through a door at the

front of the church, then downstairs and around a couple of corners to a room with shelves of toys and kids' pictures on the wall. A day care. Across the hall was a gym. The church smell was fainter down here.

"Will you be all right now?" asked the sad man. "I have to be going. The service will be starting soon."

"Oh, yes, thanks," said Dad over his shoulder, hustling Bernie toward the bathroom.

Time passed, but not much else. Dad said encouraging things to Bernie, and Bernie tried hard, but it looked like the tiger didn't want to come to the water hole after all. Bill and I checked out the toys, which all had that day-care appearance. Used, but not loved. Stand-ins for the real toys at home. Bill and I wandered across the hall to the gym, which had such a low ceiling that the basketball hoops were close to the ground. I grabbed a ball – smaller than a real basketball – walked over to one of the nets, jumped up, and stuffed it in. It felt good.

"Hey!" said Bill. I passed to him. He dribbled down-court and stuffed the ball in the net at the other end.

We grinned at each other.

For the next few minutes we shot hoops. Mostly we stayed close to the baskets, dunking the ball. One-handed, two-handed, backward, on the run, spinning. It was great. Fantasy basketball. We threw alley-oop passes to each other, cramming the orange plastic sphere through the corded miniature hoops in feats of impossible, superhuman control. By the time Dad and

Bernie showed up, we must have scored three hundred points each.

"Oh. There you are," said Dad dully. "Come on, now. The service is about to start."

"Let me play," said Bernie in a loud voice.

"No, honey, we have to go," said Dad.

"I don't want to go," said Bernie. "I don't have to go."

"I know," said Dad. "Believe me, I know."

A deep sound came from – hard to say where it came from. It seemed like it came from all around us. The ceiling above us shook, and so did the floor below us. The pipes on the wall rattled. Not a loud sound, but incredibly low. As if the earth itself was speaking.

"Come on," said Dad. "That's the organ. The service is starting."

We hurried back the way we came, but the passage-ways in the church basement wound around and around like a maze, and before long we were lost. We went up some stairs, down a corridor. At the end of the corridor was another flight of stairs. Nowhere to go but up, so up we went. Dad was carrying Bernie by now.

"Well, now, hello there. Mr. Peeler, isn't that right?"

Who was he? An old man in a funeral suit. I knew him, but couldn't tell from where. Behind him, through a doorway, I could see rows of seats, and the church ceiling.

"Oh, hello," said Dad. He didn't recognize the man either. It was the tone of voice he uses when he doesn't recognize someone. "Nice to see you."

The organ was playing and people were singing.

"So sad about Tobias," said the man.

"Oh, yes," said Dad.

"I didn't know you knew him."

"Well," said Dad.

"Quite a coincidence, you knowing him."

"Ah," said Dad.

The organ stopped. Silence in the church. "The service is about to begin," said the man in a whisper. "There are some seats near the railing. You'll be able to see my wife when she gives her address."

"Oh, good," said Dad faintly.

We were up high, in a balcony that went all the way around the church, looking down on everyone in the congregation. Bernie was in Dad's lap, wriggling faintly. Bill and I sat next to each other.

The church was stuffed with good clothes, like a steamer trunk on the first-class deck. Suits and ties and dresses in the pews. Military uniforms with gold braid up and down the aisles and beside the doors. Red-and-white robes in the choir stalls. Black-and-white robes in front of the microphone. I felt awkward in my shorts and sandals. I pulled my T-shirt down to cover my knees.

But the awkwardness couldn't cover up my sense of accomplishment. It had been worth all the effort bring-ing Marty here. I felt satisfied, as if I'd done a good thing. I was proud of myself. A good feeling, and not all that common.

"How do you feel, Bill?" I asked. "Are you glad Marty's here?"

"Where is he?" said Bill. "I can't see him or Grandma."

The man in the black-and-white robes was tall and dignified, with – very visible from the balcony – a small and perfectly circular bald spot in the middle of his head. "My friends, this is a happy occasion," he said, surprising me, since he looked like he was on the verge of tears. Then he explained. "Happy for Tobias Oberdorf, who has been called up to heaven with a merry noise. But for the rest of us, left behind in this vale of sorrow, for his friends and colleagues, and especially for his family, it is a time of profound grief and longing."

When he mentioned the family, the speaker turned his head to indicate a group of men, women, and children who sat next to him, facing everyone else, the way speakers and special guests sit onstage at a school assembly. The family. Marty's family.

They were mostly old, mostly wearing black, mostly still. A few exceptions were a girl and a boy about my age, a lady in a purple and red dress, with a big hat, and the fattest man I had ever seen, who squirmed most uncomfortably on a front-row chair that wasn't nearly big enough for him.

I didn't see Marty. I looked around the congregation carefully, taking it from the back and searching all the rows up to the front. I checked all around the balcony.

A familiar old lady was talking now. Black dress, white hair. She'd been sitting onstage near the girl, who was trying not to yawn. The old lady called the congregation her friends, too. "My husband and I were on vacation in Canada two days ago," she said, "when we happened upon a copy of a New York newspaper in our hotel room. An earlier guest had left it behind. Chance, you might think. But not I. It was not chance that forgot to clean out our wastebasket. It was not by chance that I glanced down at the obituary page. No, my friends, it was . . ." – I turned to Bill, my mouth wide open – ". . . the Hand of God."

"Her!" I whispered. I looked back over my shoulder at the old guy who had led us in here. "And him," I whispered. Bill nodded.

Myrna and Henry – the generous old couple we had left at the lakeside picnic spot without donuts. *This* was their church.

Myrna had a lot more to say, but I soon found my attention wandering. I kept looking for Marty and Grandma, and couldn't see them. I noticed a plaque on the wall behind me, which said that Mary Ann somebody or other had departed this life in 1825, in her seventh year; I couldn't decide if she was older than I was, or not. She was either a hundred and eighty, or seven.

The service dragged a bit. Bernie wriggled off Dad's lap and tried to fling himself over the railing. "Thanks," Dad whispered to a lady with piled-up hair and fast reflexes. I found another plaque to read. Susan had been cut down in the flower of youth – mind you, no one puts up a plaque if you're still alive.

At last I saw Grandma. She was staring up at us, probably because of Bernie. She was sitting toward the back of the church, with a face like thunder. I knew better than to wave in church, but I nodded my head in her direction. She nodded back, but she still looked furious.

Marty was not sitting beside her. Marty didn't seem to be anywhere in the church.

"There's Grandma," I told Bill. "But where's Marty?"

17

Make a Noise

The organ played something I knew. "Amazing Grace! How sweet the sound! That . . ." something, something, something. People stood up to sing, and stayed standing even after the hymn was over.

"Come on," Dad said, heading for the archway, Bernie in his arms. Below, people were filing slowly down the aisles. The organ was playing something else.

We met up with Grandma at the bottom of the stairs. People were milling all around us. Lots of conversation. Not a lot of laughter. Grandma was still upset. "I thought everyone had disappeared on me," she said.

"Where's Marty?" I asked her right away.

She shook her head. "I don't know. He ran off," she said. "We got to the front door of the church and he saw a lady in a big hat and he started to tremble. 'I can't do it,' he said, over and over, and bolted."

"Poor guy," said Dad. "Oh, excuse me," he said to a woman who was pushing past us. We moved a little farther down the hall. The church smell was still there, but it was accompanied by another familiar smell. Bill recognized it, too. His eyes lit up. "Chocolate," he said.

I felt like an overloaded computer. *Function error, probably insufficient memory to process data.* I felt sorry for Marty, of course, but I was also mad at him. Ungrateful, that's what he was. After all the trouble we'd taken to get him here. My feeling of accomplishment went *phut!*

"Let's go," I said. Suddenly I was struck by a picture of Mom waiting for us at Auntie Vera's – all dressed up to go to dinner. "Let's leave right now."

But by then we had already drifted farther down the hall, borne along by a tide of well-dressed bodies that kept pushing us onward, a current of Oberdorfs and friends of Oberdorfs, who carried us downstream with them. And more bodies came bumping into us, even now, pushing us closer and closer to –

"There you are! Isn't this providential!"

Myrna, of course. She came right over to us and put her arm around my shoulders. "Henry told me that you'd come! I am so glad, so very glad!" Myrna couldn't hear of us going just yet. Or maybe she just couldn't hear. We tried to tell her, but she pushed along with the rest of the congregation, and soon we found ourselves in a large room filled with people standing around, drinking coffee and eating dessert.

"You must know Marie," she said. "Let me find her for you."

"Actually," said Dad, "we –"

"There she is. Oh, Marie!" Myrna waved. Marie was the lady in the hat and striped dress. Tobias's wife – widow, I guess, now. The man in the black-and-white robes had spoken very feelingly about her. A nice woman, apparently.

"Um," said Dad. He tried to wrestle free of Myrna's grasp, but she had a grip of iron as well as bad ears. He was led away, trailing Grandma like clouds of glory.

Ham! I said to myself.

Bill and Bernie weren't upset. Was it an awful fate to be abandoned in a roomful of dessert? Bill licked his lips. Bernie stood on tiptoe to see better. I could understand their point of view. But I was so disappointed about Marty, I almost didn't have an appetite.

We found ourselves behind the very fat man. All three of us. His dark suit was wide enough to block our view of the food table. I peeped around the back of his coat, and saw squares and cookies and triangle sandwiches. When he'd finished loading up, it was our turn.

The noise level rose around us like water in a bathtub. The fat man ate busily. So did we. Bernie had a Rice Crispie square in each hand, and was taking alternating bites. Bill grinned around a mouthful of chocolate chip cookie. "Not bad, eh?" he whispered.

"Not too bad." But it wasn't really good either. Marty should have been there, not us. We didn't belong. And time was marching on. It was three o'clock. The sooner we left the better. I wanted a chance to have a bath, maybe have Mom fix my hair. I tried to smile when Myrna came back, but it wasn't my best smile.

"Jane, Jane, come with me! There's someone I want you to meet." Somehow Myrna being so happy to see us made it worse, not better. "You boys come along, too," she said.

She grabbed the arm that wasn't full of dessert and propelled me forward. Bernie and Bill followed, munching doubtfully. She led us up to a family group – a woman, a boy, and a girl. I'd noticed the girl during the service, yawning. Part of the family.

Myrna introduced her daughter, Mrs. Stouffer. The girl and boy were her children, Myrna's grandchildren. Emma, the granddaughter, was the one I was supposed to have so much in common with. "Hi," I said to her. She kept her hands together, so I gave a small hello wave.

She unclasped her hands. "Bye," she said, waving back.

"Now, Emma," said her mom. "Don't tease the girl. She's not used to you."

"Excuse me?" I said.

"There's no excuse for you," said Emma quickly.

Her mom laughed. Myrna smiled and moved off, now that the two of us were getting along so well.

"Ha, ha," I tried to smile. "That's a good one. Very sharp."

"Not like you, then."

"What?"

Emma grinned. "You're very dull."

"Oh?" I said. And stopped.

"Emma," said her mom warningly. Her brother – who'd been introduced as an afterthought – looked blank.

She was a little taller than I am, and a lot ruder. Her dark hair was cut close to her head. Her dress hung on her skinny shoulders like a set of drapes. Her chin bent to one side, like her mom's. Like Marty's, come to think of it.

Emma sneered. "Why don't you make a noise like an airplane and take off," she said.

Her mom snickered. "Emma, stop that. You're such a tease."

Bill said, quietly, "Let's go."

"Emma's so clever," her mom went on. "We're used to her, but she oughtn't to be rude to strangers. She just does it to show off her high spirits and intellect."

Emma made a face at me. High spirits.

"That's okay," I said. "No hard feelings, Emma. One of these days you'll make a noise like a tree and grow up."

Emma's head snapped back as if I'd closed a door in her face. "Why don't you make a noise like snow, and melt away."

Her mom laughed, but not very hard. "Snow . . . melt away. Very good, Emma."

"You're kidding," I said to Emma's mom. "You call that good?"

"Don't say anything," she replied. "It's better not to try. She'll only get worse. And really, her insults are so amusing."

Emma opened her mouth again. I should just have gone. I shouldn't even have stayed this long. But I couldn't help myself. I spoke fast. "Why don't you make a noise like a dead bird and get stuffed," I said. Emma closed her mouth. I kept going. "Why don't you make a noise like a golf ball and fall in a hole."

Behind me, Bill spluttered. Emma's mom didn't say anything.

Emma took a step back. High spirits indeed. The girl was a bully. "You should go to the store so you can get a new outfit," she said.

"You should believe in reincarnation so you can get a new life," I said.

Emma's face worked a bit. I guess she wasn't used to people fighting back. "Your hair reminds me of the sunset," she spat. "Too bad it can't sink below the horizon."

My hair again. At least she'd noticed it. "Funny. I was just thinking that your hair was like a winter's day: short, dark, and dirty."

Bullies are all or nothing, like balloons. They look great when they're complete, but once you prick them they disappear. Emma knew she couldn't bully me, so she just stopped. She stood there staring at me, and I could see the angry spark in her eyes go out. She was still angry – but not at me anymore. It was the same with Greg, in grade three. I knocked him down, and then he got up and ran away across the school yard, hitting himself.

I hadn't liked that part of the confrontation with Greg, and I didn't like it now with Emma. I'd had enough of the game. "Your personality, Emma, has all the charm of the common cold," I said. "Unfortunately, it seems to be just as contagious." I smiled. "I'm sorry for insulting you. Actually, your hair looks very pretty. And that's a nice dress."

She didn't say anything. I went on.

"I'm sorry to hear about Mr. Oberdorf. I didn't know him, but he sure sounds like a nice man. I know his brother, Martin. Have you tried these chocolate squares? They're good."

She opened her mouth, but no insult came out of it. It was as if she'd forgotten how to speak nicely. She might have wanted to, but it was a foreign language.

A man with a camera around his neck came up and whispered in Emma's mom's ear.

"Okay," she said to him. "Emma, darling, we have to go. There's going to be a picture."

"It was nice to meet you," I said. I waved again. "This time I do mean good-bye."

Emma followed her mother without another word. The brother hadn't said anything the whole time. Before following his family, he leaned forward and put out his hand. Feeling a little ashamed of myself, I took it.

Bernie was licking his fingers. "That was a mean girl," he commented calmly.

"Not as mean as Jane," said Bill in admiration.

We found Dad and Grandma with Henry. "They're lining up the family for a group photograph," said Henry. "Under the chandelier."

Emma and her brother and mom were at the end of the line. Not one of them was speaking. Myrna stood next to them. The very fat man was having trouble finding a place where he wouldn't block someone's line of sight. He hung on to a brownie like a life preserver.

Henry shook his head sadly. "Poor Cousin Joe. Would you believe he was once a bodybuilder? Fifteen years ago he had a perfect physique."

"What happened to Cousin Joe?" asked Grandma.

"They opened a Häagen-Dazs outlet a block over from where he lived. One night he went in and ordered a cone – macadamia nut."

My dad shook his head. "The old macadamia nut. A killer."

The photographer had everyone lined up now. He backed up a bit, twisted this way and that, and asked everyone to look at him. He didn't ask them to say cheese – that was for weddings.

The kid in the middle of the row was really upset. He wouldn't look at the camera. Marie stood next to him. She was talking to him, and he was shaking his head. A shy kid, I thought.

And then I caught a whiff of a familiar scent. Not Summer Nights.

Mothballs.

And Marie put her arm around the kid's shoulder to turn him, and the photographer snapped the picture, and I opened my mouth and cried out, "Marty!"

Not a shy kid at all. A small man overwhelmed by huge emotions. An older man, long estranged from his family, who had, it seemed, come home at last.

18

"Not Again!"

Marty had been stuck behind Cousin Joe during the service, which explained why I hadn't been able to see him. "I ran right into the big guy on the church steps," he told us, "and he recognized me right away. Picked me up like a baby and carried me around to the side entrance. Big Joe. Imagine, I used to let him beat me at arm wrestling when he was a kid."

We were saying our good-byes in front of the church, under a sky that threatened but didn't mean it yet, like your parents when you wake them up too early on Christmas morning. Marie and Myrna and Henry and Cousin Joe and a couple of other old people I didn't know stood in a semicircle and waved at us. Marty was shaking everyone's hands, one after the other.

Did he look like he belonged? I couldn't tell. Not entirely. His long-nailed fingers looked different from theirs. His clothes smelled different. His eyes seemed to go deeper inside his head than theirs did. His smile came and went. Mind you, one of the old men there had a sideways pointing chin like Marty's, or Emma's. An Oberdorf chin. Not often you see something as obvious as that. My friend Bridget claims to have her mom's eyes, but I can't see it at all. They're bright blue, is all, just like a lot of people's. Just like Barbie's, I told her – but Bridget didn't seem delighted to have a doll's eyes.

Did Marty look happy? I couldn't tell that either.

My hand got an extra-long squeeze. So did Grandma's. Then he turned and went back to his family semicircle. Marie and Joe made room between them.

Thick gray clouds were ganging up on the sun as we walked to the van. Bernie was sitting on Dad's shoulders and holding my hand. Affectionate. "Marty's fingernails are almost as long as Auntie Vera's," he said.

"I suppose they are," I said.

"There are seven windows on one side of the church," he said, "and seven on the other."

"Really? I didn't notice," I said.

"Daddy's and my shadow is bigger than yours," he said. But then the clouds moved in, and the sun disappeared, taking our shadows with it.

"Not anymore," I said.

The van was about halfway down the block. Not a bad parking spot, an hour and a half ago. Mind you, there hadn't been a police officer standing in front of it then. There was now.

"Not again!" said Dad. He dashed across the street, Bernie bouncing around on his head like a badly tied bonnet. "No!" he shouted. "Stop! Wait!"

Did the police officer look up when Dad came running over? Did she stop writing? She did not.

"Ham!" said Grandma. "What can we do?" She was upset that Dad was getting a ticket.

She hadn't cared yesterday.

I looked at Grandma – an old woman, walking slowly. An idea bit me.

"Limp," I said.

"What?"

"Limp, Grandma. And lean on Bill and me."

"I can walk just fine – Oh." She got it. She put out her hand. I grabbed it.

"What a nice girl you are, Jane," she said in a quavery voice, "to help your frail old Grandma."

I smiled. "And what a nice Grandma you are."

"I'm glad you're with me, Jane."

"And I'm glad to be with you, Grandma."

Funny thing, we were both pretending; and at the same time we weren't pretending. I wonder if there's a word for that.

"You know," I said, not pretending at all, "I wouldn't mind coming to visit you sometime. When we get back home."

She squeezed my hand. "You know," she said. "I wouldn't mind you coming to visit."

"I'm the only girl at our place," I said. "Usually."

"Me, too," she said.

I thought back to the man with the hole in his heart, who pulled the baby from the inferno. You know, when the doctors examined him after the rescue, they couldn't find anything wrong with him. The hole had just closed up. A miracle, the article said. Did I believe in miracles?

"Come on, you idiot," I whispered to Bill. "Take Grandma's other arm."

We crossed the street three abreast, and very slowly.

"Oh, there you are, Alexander. I came as fast as I could."

She sounded so nice.

"Come along, you dear little tots," she said to us, trying to open the door of the van. I rushed to help her. Grandma leaned against the open door and breathed deeply. "I would have come sooner, but with my bad leg, I can't walk as fast as I used to." Her voice was quite faint.

"What is wrong with Grandma?" whispered Bernie.

"Nothing," I whispered. "Nothing at all."

She addressed the policewoman. "I am sorry Alexander parked here in the NO PARKING zone. It's my fault. We were invited to the memorial service at the church, and I can't walk as far as I used to."

The policewoman cleared her throat. "Well, ma'am," she began.

"Alexander is my son-in-law. He's taking me to visit my other daughter in Massachusetts. I haven't seen her in . . . so long." Grandma swallowed. "And what a journey it's been. Children disappearing, misadventures in our hotel, breakdowns by the side of the road . . . I don't know how much strength I have left. Oh, Jane, dear?" She swallowed again, and turned slowly, an expression of patience and long-suffering on her face.

"Yes, Grandma," I said.

"Could you help your poor crippled grandmother into the van, honey?"

I opened the sliding door and held out my arm.

"Here, ma'am." The policewoman stepped in front of me and helped Grandma into the van. "Allow me."

"Why, thank you, young lady," said Grandma. "Thank you very much."

"My privilege," said the policewoman.

"Ah. That's better. You have a mother yourself, don't you, my dear," said Grandma.

"Yes, ma'am."

"And you're very kind to her, aren't you?"

The policewoman blinked. "I will be," she said. "I will be from now on. Listen, can I show you good folks the way back to the highway?"

"Thank you," said Dad.

The policewoman took a city map out of her uniform pocket and marked the route in thick black pen. Dad started to thank her through the open window, and stopped when she handed him the ticket.

"Oh," said Dad.

"Parking in a marked NO PARKING zone. Fifty-four dollars."

"Hey," said Grandma.

The policewoman shrugged. "Doing my job," she said.

"Very conscientious," said Dad.

"Have a nice day now," said the policewoman.

"I hope your mother's proud of you!" muttered Grandma.

19

Whatever Moxie Was

I was in the backseat with the map on my knee, folded to exactly the right place. Grandma was beside me; she said she enjoyed seeing the countryside from back there. I wondered if, maybe, she missed her companion of this morning; certainly the lingering scent of moth and Marty clung tenderly to our upholstery. Anyway, Bill was in the front seat beside Dad, asking if we were there yet every few minutes and, in between times, reliving his sojourn in the Land of the Dead Oberdorfs, as he called Schenectady. Bernie was in the middle seat, asleep.

At the state line Dad followed the left-hand lane, which meant that the passenger-side window was next to the automated money collector. He gave some change to Bill and told him to deposit it.

"Wilco!" Bill had to lean out the window and reach up to drop the money in the slot. The machine whirred and clicked, and then a mechanical voice said, "Thank you. Please deposit an additional seventy-five cents."

Bill's eyes lit up like the buttons on the machine. "A talking tollbooth!" he whispered, and then, in a louder voice, "Certainly, Mr. Collector. Please stand by."

Dad was fumbling in his pocket for some more change. "Here you go," he said.

"This is Captain Billy Stardust, requesting permission to enter your territory!" Bill dropped the assortment of change into the slot. The machine whirred and clicked as before. Then the same mechanical voice said, "Thank you. Please deposit an additional seventy-five cents."

Dad had no more change. Grandma pulled out her purse and found three quarters. "Here, William," she said, handing the money forward.

He reached out the window. "We come in peace," he said slowly. "We wish no harm to you or any of your citizens." He dropped the money in, coin by coin.

"Please deposit another seventy-five cents."

"The United States is the richest country in the world," I said to Grandma.

"And now we know how it got that way," she replied.

"I wonder what would happen if we just went ahead?" I said.

There was no arm across the front of the van, like at a train crossing. Nothing to stop us from driving right past the booth, except the power of the polite mechanical voice. Dad put the car in gear. "Sorry," said Bill to the machine as we pulled ahead, "but we're out of money."

"Welcome to Massachusetts," said the machine. "Please enjoy your stay."

A storm cloud was sailing beside us like a consort battleship when I checked my watch one last time – five ten. We'd be there in a few minutes. I was probably too late for a bath, but Mom and I would get to the restaurant and the show on time.

The land rolled gently, fields on one side of the highway, and grass and white fence rails on the other. Up ahead, a dark and motionless figure caught my eye. Crooked, solitary, dressed in rags, he stood in the field of corn. One hand was raised. Was he asking us to stop? We didn't stop.

A crow flew out of the cornfield and landed clumsily on top of the figure's head. I could see what it was now – a scarecrow. We drove by in silence.

Bernie woke up, yawning. "Are we there yet?" he asked.

"Soon," said Dad.

The highway wound its way up a hillside. Thunder rolled on the right. The sky was filled with gloomy menace. And then, from the middle of the dark cloud ahead, a ray of sunlight stabbed downward. We reached the top of the hill. For a second, the van was filled with golden light. A miracle.

"Wow," I said.

Grandma smiled at me. "For a moment there the whole van was the same color as your hair, Jane."

Was she making fun of me? Evidently not.

"It looks great," she said. "Your hair, I mean. It's a lot like you. Full of moxie."

Whatever moxie was. "It's supposed to be chestnut," I said. "But I'm thinking that, maybe, it's not exactly right for me. My friend Bridget kept the purple dye – maybe we'll try that when I get home. That one's called Funky Twilight."

Now Grandma laughed. Not mean laughter. She actually sounded amused. "I want to see it," she said. "I want to see you and your . . . funky twilight hair!" Her face fell apart as she laughed, wrinkles flying all over the place. "Whew," she said, getting her breath back.

"Gesundheit," said Bernie, proudly.

A raindrop hit the windshield and trickled down. Then two more. Then a lot.

"Are we there yet?" asked Bill.

"As a matter of fact," said Dad, turning down a familiar driveway, "we are."